THE LISTENING FOREST

Other recent Avalon titles
by Marjorie Everitt:

Small Details

Country Blues

Somewhere Near Paradise

THE LISTENING FOREST

•

MARJORIE EVERITT

AVALON BOOKS

THOMAS BOUREGY AND COMPANY, INC.

401 LAFAYETTE STREET

NEW YORK, NEW YORK 10003

PRINTED IN THE UNITED STATES OF AMERICA
ON ACID-FREE PAPER
BY HADDON CRAFTSMEN, SCRANTON, PENNSYLVANIA

Prologue

It had been a quiet afternoon, with time for contemplation, full of gulls' cries and the lapping of gentle waves on the shore. Full of a natural peace.

Until the wind changed, and with it came an unnatural death that changed that peace into a living nightmare.

The wonderful incandescent sapphire streaking the waters off the northern shore of Lake Superior had dulled to a steel blue, and full-bellied clouds, purple-gray and silently ominous, had drifted in from the west with an unexpectedness that took me off guard. I'd been so intent on playing fetch-the-stick with my big mutt Boze that I hadn't noticed the change in the air, hadn't felt the breeze turn chill.

I called the lumbering, big-footed dog back to my side. It was time to go back to the gloomy, big, overgrown family summer home, time to settle in for the evening beside the comforting crackle of a warm fire, a fire that should chase the lingering shadows and shades from the corners of the high-ceilinged rooms.

In spite of the storm warnings that whipped the air around me, I felt a rather fragile contentment for the first time since—since spring. Had it been that long?

It was spring when Mother died, leaving me as sole heir to the big house in the north woods—the white elephant, I called it privately, although it was a faded and blistered ochre rather than white. And then I had suddenly been knocked flat by a bout with mononucleosis, which I'd thought was a disease specifically and diabolically designed to bedevil high school and college students.

And here it was, already late summer—or early autumn, depending on how one wanted to look at it—and a storm was rising in the west. . . .

I felt a little like a fish out of water. I was on leave of absence as executive assistant manager of one of the biggest hotels in Minneapolis, used to bright lights and hordes of people and eternal busyness. Used to reliable air-conditioning and heating and plumbing—a maintenance crew at my beck and call—and I was trying to figure out what to do with one of the biggest Victorian summer homes on the north shore of Lake Superior. Right now, I was wondering whether the aged roof of The Birches could handle a deluge. And this was supposed to be a restful retreat?

Still, I loved the eccentric old house, even though it had a strange atmosphere about it, as if I weren't quite alone in it, as if it were watching me . . . all of which was no doubt the imagination of an overworked, overstressed city woman. So I told myself, anyway.

A sudden gust of wind tangled strands of hair across my face. I tucked them under the collar of my jeans jacket, shivering a little. The same wind took an eddy of leaves across the rocky shore, and Boze whirled after them, howling with delight.

Grabbing for him, I thought I saw a movement at the top of the looming bluff behind me—just a hint of something that didn't seem to be a wind-tossed branch. I hesitated, looking up.

Nothing. A deer, perhaps, or a leaf-devil dancing in the wind. I was holding the dog's collar, slightly off-balance, when I heard the scream: a choked thin wail of terror that cut the air with an eerie sharpness, then the ugly, heart-stopping sound of something hitting the rough shore on the far side of the boulders that piled as if strewn by a giant's hand along the water's edge.

I stood still once again, trying to regain my balance, frozen by horror. Terrified screams vibrated in the air around me, bouncing off the cliffs and echoing like banshee wails. Even the wind seemed to fall silent to listen, and the wavelets tiptoed along the shore, momentarily overwhelmed by the sounds of fear.

It wasn't until I closed my eyes and tried to catch my breath that I realized that the screams were my own.

There was nothing but a dead silence on the other side of the boulders.

Chapter One

"Just for the record, Miss, your full name and address?"

"Meg—Margaret Ann Livingston," I said, pushing a stray lock of hair off my forehead with hands that still shook slightly. "I've been staying at The Birches, the old house by Birchleaf Lake, for the past two days."

It had been an hour ago—a lifetime ago—that Boze and I had been playing along the rocky shore. Playing like children, innocent and content.

It all seemed like a dark nightmare now; I'd edged with pounding heart toward the shapeless bundle splayed silently on the rocks, knowing, without looking too closely, that it was a lifeless bundle. Boze had hung back, whimpering, his head low and the whites of his eyes showing at the edges. The woman was undoubtedly dead, her head bent at a sickening angle, sightless eyes staring toward the lowering clouds.

Somehow I'd scrabbled up the steep path toward the top of the cliff, calling for help—screaming for help might be more accurate. Somehow I'd reached the top and found living people. They'd taken over and led me away from the cliff.

And now I was in the center of a subdued group gathered in The Red Finn's Inn, a hundred yards along the bluff above the spot where the accident had happened. The sheriff was there, and Red Kaarinen—the proprietor—and his wife, and a doctor, the poor woman's husband and son, and people I didn't know. . . .

A woman was dead, and the county ambulance had taken her away, and the peace was gone forever from the day.

Outside, a few drops of wind-driven rain spattered like pebbles at the windows. Boze lay huddled out on the wide veranda close to the door, looking woebegone. I knew just how he felt.

The sheriff—his name was Jack Darling, of all things— looked up from his notebook sympathetically. "Easy," he said. I'd probably unconsciously whimpered, just like Boze. "Get her a brandy, would you, Red? She needs something to warm her inside."

"Aquavit would varm her better," Red said. "Right, Dr. Chase?"

"Tea," the tall man who was a doctor said, with a firm note of authority. "Good hot tea, with sugar, Edina." The tiny aproned woman hovering at the end of the counter nodded approvingly at him and hustled off to the kitchen.

I looked up at him gratefully. I was quite sure I couldn't possibly handle anything stronger at that point. He looked back at me, levelly, unsmiling eyes dark with what might be compassion or just sternness.

"The Birches," Sheriff Darling said. "Renting the place for a few weeks?" Edina Kaarinen put the steaming tea down in front of me, and I took a scalding sip, shaking my head slightly both at the shock of the intense heat and at the question.

"It's my family's place. My third great-grandfather built the house." Facts to overlay the vision of a portly woman screaming her way off a cliff. I glanced around the dimly lit bar and grill. Figures that seemed almost unreal sat or stood in a shadowy tableau around the room, watching and listening.

I supposed the sheriff had to fit me into the picture in his own way, to verify who I was and what I was doing there. After all, I was a stranger in the village; I hadn't spent much time at The Birches since my childhood.

"Nobody there much anymore, since the old folks died a few years back," Jack Darling said flatly, almost accusingly—as if I'd been neglecting the sprawling old place. "Some people call it the haunted house, you know." I knew, but I said nothing, just stared at him. Our family ghosts were none of his business.

He was still making copious notes. I was exhausted. Couldn't he just let me go home—home to that cozy fire I'd envisioned a while ago—and, I suspected, to a probable shaking and crying fit once I got there?

"Nice old place, though," he said, looking up finally with something like approval. Probably the fact that I was a descendent of Henry Middlefield lent credence to my story.

One of the gray figures in the silent tableau moved at last, toward me, pulling one of the chairs close to me. "Are you sure you're all right?" the doctor asked, sliding his long legs under the table and speaking in a low voice. Well, of course I wasn't all right. It was a ridiculous question. I almost told him so.

Then I gave myself a mental shake and sat very straight, giving the man what I hoped was a strong and steady look. "Just a little shocked, but I'm fine, thank you. After all, I'm not the one who fell off the cliff."

He had very dark eyes, and dark, almost black, longish hair. And a cool and detached air that seemed to speak of an underlying strength. One ironic eyebrow twitched upward at my words, but he said nothing more.

Something had changed in the room with his movement

toward my table; others were moving slightly, and I felt a sudden peculiar chill that came from deep inside me. The room seemed to whirl slightly with the ghostlike movements of the others: it had to be reaction to the accident. Yet it seemed it was something more—a premonition? A long-buried memory? Something about accidents, and death—it faded as quickly as it had arisen.

"And, dammit, you didn't see or hear anything at all until she fell? How could it happen, anyway? Should be fences there. Should be posted. I told her not to go too close to the edges of those cliffs. Dangerous, I said. And her with her dizzy spells, but she wouldn't listen."

The husband. A paunchy man in his late fifties, he didn't act precisely grief-stricken. I tried to reserve judgment: at a time of tragedy, people sometimes act in peculiar ways.

I looked away from him, not answering. Nothing seemed to penetrate the heavy veil of unreality around me. I wanted to walk out the door, turn my back on the afternoon's horror, take the adoring and unquestioning Boze and disappear in the rain of the September afternoon and never come back—go back to Minneapolis, where it was civilized and one could get killed in a more ordinary way, such as being struck by an ordinary drunken hit-and-run driver while crossing an ordinary street.

"Now, Dad. Don't, Dad." The odd, crumpled-looking man with the tear-streaked face—in his mid-twenties, I guessed—must be the man's son. I began to see the other figures in the room as individual people: the still stern-faced doctor; Big Red Kaarinen, standing beside his tiny wife Edina. A tourist-type or two, looking as if they'd stepped out of the pages of L. L. Bean.

Live people now, saying expected things.

"Too bad." The good-looking blond man in the greenish windbreaker and black turtleneck looked sympathetically from Doris Taylor's husband to her son and then at me. "Really a shame." His eyes were kind, and I was grateful for his understanding glance. "It was a terrible thing to have happen," he said to Taylor. "If there's anything any of us can do—"

"Little late for that," Taylor grumbled.

Just a naturally unpleasant man, I thought, and moved my gaze down to my teacup.

"I'll get you some more tea," Edina offered softly, but I shook my head.

"Aquavit be better," Red said stubbornly. I continued to shake my head.

Giving up on me, Red moved over to Sam Taylor. "Here, then, drink this." Red put a drink in front of Sam Taylor, looking askance at the son. I wondered if it was aquavit. "You vant a drink, too, yah?"

"No. He doesn't drink." But the elder Taylor obviously did, downing the offering without drawing breath. "Stupid thing to happen, anyway," he said. It surely wasn't aquavit, or he wouldn't have been able to speak so soon.

"Not stupid, just unfortunate." The doctor transferred his cool gaze from me to Taylor, frowning a little. "Look, Mr. Taylor, maybe you and your son should go back to the inn." His dark eyes were still deep and unreadable. "You can make whatever phone calls are necessary and get some rest. It would be good for both of you."

"Phaugh." Taylor slammed his glass down and glared collectively at everyone in the room, face red and somewhat bulbous nose twitching. "Don't be surprised if I call my attorney about all this. Negligence, no doubt about it. It's a wonder somebody else hasn't been killed up there. Come on, Otis, there's no sense in staying here."

"Mama's gone." It was a small child's wail, and I realized in that instant that the younger Taylor's mental age had never kept up with his physical growth. Poor thing, I thought, and glanced back at the doctor.

Dr. Chase, Red had called him. Would he suggest a tranquilizer or sedative for the man-boy? But he was just looking sympathetically at Otis, who trailed his father disconsolately from the barroom. I felt a little sting of anger that he didn't offer any help at all.

Out on the veranda, Boze let his own feelings be known with a couple of sharp barks, and then fell patiently silent again as the Taylors' car pulled away.

It seemed as if an unheard collective sigh of relief changed the atmosphere of the big room with the Taylors' departure.

"Geez," the blond man in the windbreaker said with a lopsided grin. "If that bonchcad didn't have himself an ironclad alibi, I'd swear he pushed her off himself. Did you ever see such heartfelt grief, such sorrow?"

"Alibi?" I asked. I had to admit that suspicions had drifted across my own mind, though I'd tried to squelch them as mean-spirited and uncharitable. Sympathy for what the muddled and sorrowing Otis must be feeling made me swallow a lump in my throat.

"Lucky for him, maybe, yes, he has one." The blond man walked over to the table where the doctor, the sheriff, and I sat. "The Birches, did you say? That rambling place with the tower and all the porches? I drove past it the other day, when I was out doing a little exploring. Nice location. Must have been beautiful once—Oh, I'm Judd Patterson, incidentally. Too bad you had to get caught up in this mess."

He held out his hand, and I took it, giving him a grateful smile. His friendliness and comments about The Birches seemed so blessedly ordinary, an antidote to the gremlins of terror that still peered around the corners of my mind and heart.

Still—"You said he had an alibi?"

"Taylor had brought his dog to my office—she'd sliced the pad of her foot on something sharp," the doctor put in. "I'd just finished bandaging it up, and we came direct from there."

I blinked and frowned a little, and the—doctor?—almost smiled, catching my confusion. He didn't look as if he smiled easily. He had high cheekbones across which the skin was stretched tautly, a strong nose—a somber face. Only his eyes reflected a faint glow of humor as he looked at me.

"I'm a vet, not a regular physician. Otis—the son—came back from fishing at Bass Lake and saw all the commotion on the bluff. He knew where his father was, so they came and got him. I came along to see if I could be of any help."

"No one to help her now." Big Red spoke lugubriously, snapping his suspenders and looking solemn. Everything about the giant innkeeper was red: his hair, face, beard, suspenders, the black and crimson check of his lumberjack shirt under the voluminous denim overalls. I wondered if there were red flannels under the outerwear; I also was willing to bet that he cultivated his image very carefully, a local "character" to draw in the tourists. "Poor lady. Tsk. A shame."

As for me, I told myself, Boze and I were going to stay away from that particular stretch of cliff and rocky beach. Far away.

"I don't think there's any more information I need from you, Miss Livingston," Jack Darling was saying. He shuffled his papers into a pile, standing up. "If you think of anything that you feel I should know, you can give me a call. Think I'll just get on back to the office and make a report. Thank you, Miss Livingston."

"Meg," I corrected automatically. Boze and I should get back to the Birches, too, to that fire I'd dreamed about a lifetime ago. I didn't relish the thought of walking back in the windy rain, though it wasn't terribly far.

"Now would be a good time for that brandy," Dr. Chase said quietly. "A gloom-chaser. The worst of it's over now, and you look as if you need something more than tea. No, Red, not aquavit—brandy. One for me, too."

The others drifted away from the table, Judd Patterson with a smile and a nod. He seemed pleasant.

The brandy did warm me and chase away some of the tension. I managed to smile at the man who'd prescribed it. "Fine idea, Doctor," I told him. "I believe you were right."

"I usually am."

Well. Not just a shadow in a tableau, but a man with— was that a touch of arrogance?

"My name is Nolan," he added. "I'd be glad to drive you back to The Birches."

"Well, the walk might do me good."

He glanced at the window. "In this? No, you won't." The rain blew in thick sheets across the highway, and I could see his point, though he had an irritating way of assuming authority.

Oh, well. "All right. And thank you, Nolan Chase." I sagged a little, sighing. "It really has been the most gosh-awful, long, stinkin' afternoon I've ever spent," I murmured, downed the remainder of the fiery brandy, and closed my eyes against sudden stinging tears that threatened to overwhelm my hard-held control.

A short time later Nolan Chase guided me, one hand on my shoulder, out of The Red Finn's Inn. I had a brief moment of wanting to shake the hand off. Was it friendly? Consoling? Or something more? It felt a little, too—proprietary.

I'd managed to say good-bye in a normal way to the people we were leaving behind; I'd tried to pay Red for the tea and brandy.

He'd have none of it. "Emergency first aid," he said gruffly, snapping his suspenders and looking every inch the genial host.

I even smiled a genuine smile as I thanked him. The brandy had done its job well, in some respects. Even so, my legs still felt as if they belonged to someone else as I tried to hurry through the raindrops. The mental image of the broken body on the shore haunted the edges of my mind. I had a queasy feeling that it was emblazoned there permanently and that the horror would burn in the far corners of my memory forever.

Boze fell into step at Nolan's heels with interested willingness, jumping into the rear of the van in instant obedience to Nolan's command. Glad to get in out of the rain, I thought, though he'd largely been protected by the overhang of the veranda. The man seemed to be taking control of both me and my dog. But maybe that was what I needed, under the circumstances. . . .

"You have a way with animals," I commented as he opened the door for me.

"Have to. It's my job." I got a brief smile from him, and then he ducked around the van, dodging through the downpour that had left silvery-gray pockmarked puddles over the parking lot.

Well, yes, it was. I fastened the shoulder harness and tried to stretch away the tension in my muscles, leaning back against the seat. *Relax, Meg,* I told myself. *It's all right if he takes over. The man is trying to help you. . . .* And he did seem to be kind behind all that tight seriousness. After all, this hadn't been an afternoon that invited laughter and lightheartedness.

I quietly gave myself a good talking to. I had a built-in resentment of dominant macho males; my father had been one. In spades. He'd died when I was seven, and I'd never forgotten the almost brutal way he dominated my mother. Mother hadn't learned anything from that, apparently— she'd married a man almost as bad a few years later—and when he ran out on her, there was a series of men, all the same type.

And then her drinking, and at last her death. Mother hadn't learned from her bad choices—but *I* had. Nolan Chase's easy assumption of authority sent off red warning signals in my mind.

A dull, sodden dusk had fallen while we were in The Red Finn's. It looked as if it were set to rain, steadily and depressingly, through the night. Nolan switched on the headlights as he pulled out of the parking lot. The road wound along the edges of the sheer bluffs. Wind-driven leaves cartwheeled through the beam of the lights, to pile in a sodden mass against the barrier of rock and forest that edged the landward roadside.

He drove the way he did everything—with that flare of natural control and certainty. I shifted in my seat, glancing at his strong profile. "You know where you're going?" I asked.

"I generally do."

There he went again, although there hadn't really been any sarcasm in his voice. "I meant—do you know where The Birches is?" I wasn't going to let his slightly superior attitude get to me. After all, getting along with all kinds of people was *my* job, I reminded myself.

"I've lived here all my life. Everyone knows where the old Middlefield house is. It's practically a state historic landmark, probably the biggest 'summer cottage' ever built along the north shore. You must feel like a mouse in a cathedral, rattling around in there all by yourself.''

I had to chuckle at his description—the first inclination to laugh that I'd had in hours. "Henry Middlefield had a big family and a bigger fortune. He indulged himself. And now his 'indulgence' is in need of lots of TLC. No one's stayed there for more than a few days since my grandmother died six years ago. Granddad died in 1980, and I'm sure Nana didn't spend anything on upkeep after he was gone— the family fortune had all fizzled out years ago. And she kept herself to herself.''

He nodded. "I know. None of us knew them well.''

"At least they had some good years of retirement up here. Granddad always loved the forests and the lake. He loved to walk along the shore—''

I broke off, remembering my own walk along the shore that afternoon and wishing I hadn't brought it up.

Nolan Chase caught the sudden break in the words and shot a quick sideways look at me. "Do you mind being alone in the house tonight? I hope Jack's comment about the house being haunted didn't get to you.''

"Of course it doesn't bother me. And I have Boze," I reassured him. "I'll be fine.'' Boze gave a single sharp bark at the sound of his name, and I was suddenly very glad I'd brought the big lug with me instead of boarding him back in Minneapolis, as I'd considered. Tonight, of all nights, he was going to sleep beside my bed. He might snore, but he'd be company.

We turned at last down the narrow potholed lane that led to The Birches. Like the house, it badly needed repairs. And the forest had crowded in around it and over it, un- relentingly reclaiming its territory. The white trunks and limbs of the trees for which the house was named glowed in the growing darkness like ancient skeletons, and an army of pines had grown to impossible height and breadth, making even midday seem like dusk. I sighed deeply. What would I do with this dilapidated, broody old place, now that I'd inherited it?

Nolan picked up on the sigh immediately. "Look, maybe I shouldn't say this, but you don't look as if you'll be fine. You're pale, and your eyes look like—like—"

"Like holes in a shroud? That's what my mother used to say when I was sick."

"Descriptive, if a little gruesome." He pulled the van to a halt close to the wide veranda of The Birches, switched off the ignition, and looked skeptically from me to the house. "Maybe I'd better go in with you and make sure you have electricity. It goes off pretty often out in these outlying areas."

I looked pensively at the section of broken gutter that spilled a torrent of water over the edge of the wide porch steps. "Mmmm. I believe that. That's probably why there are a zillion kerosene lamps in the house and why Nana kept the big old wood stove in a corner of the kitchen even after they remodeled. But I don't want to take up any more of your time."

"I insist. I'd much rather take you back to Pine Lodge than leave you here in the dark without electricity or a phone."

The dark, rain-gloomed house did look pretty forbidding at this moment. "Right," I said after a brief pause. Boze was a great companion, but another human being to help check the house out might be a good idea. "Thanks. And I can fix a pot of coffee. And I made an apple pie yesterday."

"You talked me into it," he said, already halfway out of the car. He gave me a smile that brought flecks of light to his dark eyes. He opened the tailgate to let Boze out, and I had hardly a moment to decide whether I was doing the right thing.

We were on the steps when Boze shot past us, galloping with a flurry of furious barking toward the gnarled oaks at the left of the veranda. Was there a hint of movement in the thick underbrush? But no one with any sense would be out on such a night. It was just wind or a forest animal. I shouted at Boze, but it was Nolan's stronger voice that got his attention.

Or perhaps the shadow he was chasing simply disappeared—a raccoon, a deer. The muddy-pawed dog turned and paddled back toward us through the puddles with an apologetic canine smile.

"To the back porch," I told him sternly. "You'll have to be dried off before you come in the kitchen." Boze trotted resignedly toward the back of the house.

"I wonder what he was after," I mumbled, a little uneasy in spite of myself. "Darned dog," I added, pulling my house key from my jacket pocket.

"Hard to tell—probably nothing. Just shadows." But I couldn't quite agree that it was "nothing," and Nolan didn't sound too certain, either. Maybe the ghostly appearance of the old house was having its effect on us.

"Or a small animal," I tried. It sounded reasonable.

"Glad you have him with you," Nolan said, his tone of voice and his words bringing a sense of ordinary logic back. "He's a nice dog. Well-behaved."

"He has to be. He lives in a hotel, and he doesn't get a chance to chase after wild animals very often." My hand shook a little in spite of myself as I fitted the knobby, old-fashioned key into the lock. Was it a touch of apprehension or the fact that Nolan Chase seemed to be standing much closer to me than was necessary? Being protective, of course, but there really was no reason for that . . . an invasion of what I called my privacy zone tended to set off alarms.

I pushed the door open and reached for the switch. To my relief, the old-fashioned candle lights in the bronze sconces on either side of the door glowed reassuringly—though somewhat feebly—across the parquet flooring of the big hall. The graceful stairs rose, dimly visible, at the far side; everything seemed secure, if not cozy and warm.

"Gawd," Nolan said. "It's a cavern. What an atmosphere!" Right. That's one thing that The Birches always had, I thought: atmosphere. Acres of it.

"And this is just the Great Hall," I said, chuckling. He was farther away from me now—I could relax. "You should see the parlor. Go left, now, through the dining room and then back to the kitchen, and watch out for the swinging door. It sticks."

I hadn't removed the dust covers from the dining-room furniture, so it seemed that pale ghosts were watching as we slipped through the dusky rooms—more atmosphere. I flicked on lights as we went, trying to dispel the gloom, but the chill and the damp remained.

"I can put a fire in the kitchen fireplace," I said. "There's dry wood under cover on the back porch."

"I'll get it," Nolan said. "And if there are any old towels out there, I'll rub down Boze while you put on the coffee." He started toward the door that led to the small back porch while I dug under the sink for the towels.

"Here," I said, straightening and crossing the kitchen toward him. "These should do."

"Meg, did you close and lock your back door before you left?"

"Of course." I looked past him at the door. It was slightly ajar, and on the far side Boze whined impatiently. My heart skipped a beat, then thudded against my ribs. "Maybe—

maybe the lock didn't quite catch—and it was blown by the wind?''

"Maybe." We were standing close together again, and I didn't step away. At that moment I'd forgotten all about privacy zones. What had Boze been chasing out there in the twilight shadows?

I felt vulnerable and uncertain—not feelings I was used to. Nolan took the towels from me, his hand lingering on mine, his eyes catching mine for a long, hypnotic moment. A shiver ran through me, a fire and a chill that simultaneously swamped rational thought. There was some kind of dark magic in the man. . . .

Then he turned, reluctantly, and swung the door gently, watching the latch. "A little out of line, that's all. The settling of the house—All right, Boze. I'm coming." There was a faint huskiness in his voice, though the words were ordinary.

Putting the coffee on, I made a deliberate effort to still my shaking hands and think rationally. He was probably right—again—the house had settled. And I'd imagined the magic.

By the time Nolan and Boze were back in the kitchen, the rich aroma of coffee was filling the room. I sliced chunks of the pie, watching Nolan pile firewood on the hearth. He knelt, seemingly lost in thought, studying the grate, the stones of the hearth.

What a wonderful profile, I mused, then stifled the thought. "There's kindling in the box there."

"Hmmmm." It was an odd "hmmmm," one that sounded like trouble. What now? "Have you had a fire in this fireplace since you've been here?"

"No—it hasn't been chilly until today."

"Well." The "well" sounded much like the "hmmm." He stood up and shook his head. "It would be a good idea to have this one checked out before you burn in it—there are cracks along the firewall, clear out onto the hearth. Settling again, I suppose.''

I sighed. "The house needs so much. There may be leaks in the attic. And the plumbing is antediluvian, and the circuits are probably about to blow—''

"Hey, don't worry. I'm sure the house is basically solid. You could fix it up and have something really unique.''

His deliberate objectivity helped put things in perspective, at least. But—"Too darned unique for one woman and a dog. Not exactly a cozy weekend cottage. And it would be hard to sell.''

"So what *are* you going to do with it?''

"Darned if I know. Dynamite, maybe?''

Boze pushed his muzzle against my leg, then whimpered and made a circuit of the room. He still seemed restless and uneasy, and he was making me feel the same way. Nolan looked thoughtful, watching him.

"Is this place as big as it looks from the outside?''

"Bigger. Nooks and crannies and hidden stairs, and secret rooms where ghosts drift in and out at the full of the moon.''

He made a face. "Very funny. But I'm serious. I've been thinking. What with a possible leaky roof, Boze being spooked, the unlatched door, it would be a good idea if we checked out the whole place before I leave. I'm sure everything's fine, but we'd both feel better, knowing, wouldn't we?''

He was right again, darn him. "Thank you," I said, only slightly grudgingly. "That might be a good idea. And then we can have that pie and coffee, and I have ice cream. Thank goodness the power didn't go off—I just filled the freezer yesterday.''

I had to say it. As if some malevolent force were just waiting for its cue, the lights flickered twice and then died, plunging us into a sudden, enveloping darkness.

Chapter Two

"Hmmmmm." He was remarkably good at saying that. "Well. You said something earlier about it being a bad day. In fact, you put it pretty strongly. It isn't getting much better, is it?"

Somehow I'd half expected the darned electricity to go off. It just seemed as if it *should* on a day like this; I shook my head ruefully, then realized that he couldn't see me in the dark.

"There's an oil lamp on the kitchen work table," I said. "Sit still. I'll get it." I'd found it in the cabinet under the kitchen sink the day before, close to a half-used container of colored lamp oil. The kitchen, like all the rooms, had looked featureless, bare, and Spartan when I arrived. Long ago, knickknacks and decorative objects had been put in boxes, on shelves, and in drawers—and probably in the attics. I'd dragged the lamp out. It had glowed warm and homey in the middle of the work table, surrounded by pine cones I'd picked up and a handful of early fall leaves.

I hadn't realized it would be so handy—so soon. There was a box of matches in the table drawer. It only took a moment to coax a soft, flickering glow to life, and I replaced the chimney and carried the lamp to the maple center table.

"Does the power stay off for days around here? Hours? Minutes?"

"Yup," Nolan answered, none too helpfully. "All depends."

"Thanks a bunch."

"Want to go back into town to the lodge?"

"No. I'll tough it out."

In the golden lamplight I saw him shrug slightly, shadows moving across the angular planes of his face. "You might be lucky. Sometimes it's just a few minutes. I'll stick around."

"You don't have to do that." I felt slightly guilty—and there was that edge of confusion I'd felt earlier. Nolan Chase had a natural way of assuming command to which I had a natural knee-jerk negative reaction. I wanted to tell him I was capable of taking care of myself.

Yet—his presence warmed the room, taking the edge off the chill of the events of the past few hours. And I couldn't deny that underlying surge of attraction that had flared between us.

"I don't mind staying." Was he just being polite? His voice was flat, so the statement sounded coolly courteous. A touch of the chill crept back to tease my neck and shoulders with a shiver—one that seemed to have an unaccountable disappointment in it.

But then he took a deep breath and smiled, and it was as if a flame warmed flickering lights somewhere soul-deep in his eyes. "You've really had a rotten afternoon. I don't like to go away and leave you alone in the dark. Can you find another lamp? We'll check the house—maybe by then the power will be back on."

I took a deep breath of my own and looked away from those mesmerizing, light-filled eyes. "I—well, if you think we should. But I'd be okay, really. I do have Boze, and matches, and lamps."

"And eyes that look like holes in a shroud?"

He said it kindly. But—did I look that bad? I wished he'd quit telling me about it. It was helping to shred my morale into piles of useless fluff.

"Look," I told him firmly, "I'm just fine, and if you make one more remark about how bad my eyes look, I'll break this lovely lamp over your head. Which would be a shame, since it's probably a very collectible antique. The lamp, I mean. To set the record straight, I had mono after my mother died in July. I thought mono was for high school and college students, but I learned better. It's been hard to shake, so I'm up here on a leave of absence just—getting away from everything. I'm sure my eyes and the rest of me will recuperate after I've had a few days' rest and relaxation."

I paused, wondering why I was telling him more than he really needed to know. I couldn't seem to stop myself. It must be some kind of nervous reaction. "I don't think I'm doing very well at the rest and relaxation bit so far, am I?" I said ruefully.

"Hmmmm." It was a very thoughtful "hmmmm." "I'm sorry." He sounded as if he meant that. "Sounds like you've had a great year. I didn't mean to pry, incidentally." Almost as if he'd been reading my thoughts. "I'm just naturally curious—"

A sudden peculiar, loud skreaking sound at the kitchen window made him break off and made me gasp involuntarily. Mad rabid bats? Vampires? At this point, I could have believed just about anything. Eyes narrowed, Nolan scanned the darkness reflecting dimly back at us, one hand reaching out to cover my own that had clenched in startled reflex on the tabletop.

"Branch," he said succinctly. "Rubbing against the window."

"You're sure?" But of course he was right—that's what

it had sounded like, hadn't it? "Sorry. Guess I'm just on edge."

"Can't imagine why." He released my hand abruptly, as if he'd just discovered he'd covered it with his own, then reached down and gave Boze a scratch behind the ears. "Why does he live in a hotel?"

"Wha—Oh. Boze?" That's right, I remembered remarking about that. Nolan didn't miss much. I rubbed my hands together, trying to bring back the warmth. "Because he lives with me."

"And you live in a hotel?"

"I'm the assistant executive manager at the Hotel North Star in Minneapolis."

"Hmmmmm." Appreciative, this time. "Sounds impressive. They allow animals at your hotel, then. Very progressive."

I wasn't sure whether he was impressed at my glorified title or that Boze could live at the hotel. "I have an apartment in the west wing. And they do allow pets with reservations."

"You mean they have reservations about admitting pets, or that the animals have to make reservations? Never mind. I'm being facetious. But at least I made you smile a little. Now, let's find another lamp and take a look around this enormous deserted museum. Would you know if anything were missing?"

I shook my head. "I doubt it. But most of the more valuable things were either sold or packed away, and the house is so far off the beaten path that it never seems to have been bothered. We have a retired gentleman from Two Harbors come up twice a month to check it out, and he's never found any problems that I know of."

"And neither will we, I'm sure." Nolan lit the second lamp I'd dragged from the dish cupboard. Our shadows seemed to jump away in two directions against the walls, dim dancing silhouettes. "I like lamplight, don't you?"

I watched the shadows dancing on the walls and wasn't too sure that I shared his liking—at least not at this moment. "Right now it seems downright spooky. You know, I have a good strong torch flashlight somewhere. Wouldn't that be better?"

"Nope. Out of character. Lead on. Are there any skeletons in the closets?"

"Not that I know of. You may have any that we find, if you like." It was an enormous relief to feel that the atmosphere between us had lightened; I determined to keep things that way. There were no skeletons and few supplies in the small pantry—I'd have to do some more shopping. Far to the east, swelling thunder like distant drums rumbled and died away. The storm was passing.

"Do you ever think we'll know what really happened today?" I asked as we checked the butler's pantry and the shelves in the shadowy dining room. I spoke slowly, not really wanting to ask but unable to stop myself. But then maybe it would be better if I talked about it.

"Hmmmm?" He raised the lamp a bit and checked a corner cupboard. "Nothing missing here? Doesn't look as if anything's out of place—well. Jack Darling is good at his job. He'll check out the cliff—he'll check out the people involved—but I don't really think there was any foul play there. Do you?"

"No," I answered hesitantly, not really sure. Our shadows crawled along the walls of the hall, and the monotonous drip of the broken gutter outside was disturbingly loud here near the door. "She slipped, she fell—or did she jump? Living with Taylor couldn't have been easy." That possibility hadn't occurred to me before. It was a disquieting thought. "And poor Otis. I wonder what she was like . . . I wonder how she and Taylor got along. . . . ''

"We'll never know." We were in the parlor now, checking the big bay. Nothing but cobwebs, nothing but silence. He turned abruptly, brushing invisible webs from his face. His eyes looked darker and more unreadable than ever in the gloom. The deep warmth that had been there earlier was gone, and his voice had taken on a strained, hard edge, cold and reserved. What had I said or done to cool that warmth?

"Sure, there are times when you wonder why people get married," he said. "Why they stay together." He shook his head slightly. "And then there are those like Red and Edina—you can't imagine them *not* being together. So what's upstairs?''

"Lots more rooms, cobwebs, and dust. I don't think we're going to find anything, really, but thank you.''

"We're checking out the upstairs, and the attic, too. If there are any leaks, you should at least have a bucket up there.''

We were silent, climbing the stairs with Boze and our shadows close on our heels. The lamplight made strange patterns dance on the walls; long unused hinges squeaked in protest at our touch. There was nothing but dust and darkness.

Even in the attics, there were no leaks. No damage, no intruders, no problems—

"No ghosts," he said with a hint of a smile as we made our way back down the stairs.

"You expected ghosts?''

"Never know, do you?''

I didn't answer that question, walking ahead of him back into the kitchen. It was no wonder that the townspeople called this a haunted house, all things considered, but it was just that it was so isolated, so decrepit—poor old house.

I'd have to see what I could do to restore its turn-of-the-century dignity—if I had enough time and money. "Thank you for your help," I told him.

"You'll find people around here helpful and friendly. If you need anything, all you have to do is ask."

"I appreciate that. Does Judd Patterson live here, too?"

He shook his head. "Never saw him before this afternoon. Probably up for a week or so, like most of the tourists, catching the fall colors." His voice grew softer, almost caressing. "There's magic in the forests at this time of the year—a feeling in the air, a certain light—"

As if his very words had themselves worked magic, the lights in the kitchen flashed on, off, then back on—to stay, at least for the time being.

"Thank goodness." I looked across the table at Nolan and smiled. Normalcy had returned. "More pie? Coffee?"

"No, thanks." He gathered himself up, looking, I thought, slightly relieved that the electricity was back on and he could leave. "I have to get back to Kitty. I'm already late."

I blinked. Back to Kitty—why hadn't it occurred to me before that the man was probably married? As attractive as he was, it was unlikely he'd be single. I tried to ignore a tiny twinge of disappointment. After all, I hardly knew anything about the man. *He'd* been the one asking all the questions.

"Kitty," I said, rather flatly. "Your wife?"

"My—of course not." He was actually chuckling. "Kitty is Red's pet bobcat, due for a feline leukemia shot. I told him I'd stop by this evening—"

"Pet bobcat?" I said incredulously. Boze opened one eye and whuffled, staring at Nolan as if he were as unbelieving as I was. "Red has a—tame pet bobcat?"

"Well . . . as tame as you could expect of a wild animal.

I keep telling him not to be too trusting, but he's had Kitty since she was a kitten, and he likes to entertain the tourists by serving drinks with the cat lopped across his shoulders like a fur stole. It does bring in customers, I'll say that.''

"And no one messes with Red," I hazarded.

"Got it.''

We'd made our way back through the huge, brooding hall to the front door, Boze literally dogging our heels as if afraid we'd disappear into the vast darkness.

Nolan turned to me with a long, measuring look. ''You'll be all right? Being alone in this—this mausoleum doesn't bother you?''

"Of course I'll be all right. And it's not a mausoleum. It's just an oversized, once-elegant old summer home. Thanks for all your help.''

He shook his head slightly, then bent to rub the top of Boze's head. When he straightened, he'd moved a step closer to me, his eyes fixed on mine. I was acutely aware of the strong bones of his face, of the strength and energy in those deep eyes and in that lean, well-muscled body. His hair grew into a widow's peak in the center of his bronzed forehead; his brows and lashes were thick and dark—

He was an extremely vital and attractive man.

I took an involuntary step back, trying to pull my familiar protective cloak of distance around me. It didn't quite work. His eyes still held mine hypnotically.

He reached out, one finger touching my cheek. Moth wings fluttered along my spine. ''Get some rest,'' he said softly, then added ''city woman'' with a slight, puzzling change of inflection. And he was gone.

A moment later I heard his van pull away, watched the taillights fade into the depths of the crowding trees. I hadn't moved, watching the darkness of the night return, trying to sort out my feelings. Hey, I wasn't a sucker for an attractive man. Look, but don't touch . . . my mother's mistakes had subtly fashioned my attitudes. So I'd worked hard, fighting to get through school, battling for a sense of self-sufficiency and self-esteem.

It hadn't come easy. I'd stayed far away from domineering men, and Nolan Chase—well, he was close to being one of those. And I had work to do here and back in Minneapolis and no time for yearning after a bossy backwoods vet who should have a sticker pasted on his forehead reading *Typical Male Ego*.

I must remember that. Yet something in the way he'd looked at me. . . . Embers of the fire I'd felt earlier flared up again, and I turned my mind deliberately from Nolan Chase, calling Boze to my side and scanning the dark woodlands once more before going in.

The forest reached crooked branch-fingers up to the edges of the house, dark but not quite silent, watching and listening. Drops of moisture pattered lightly from branches and leaves. From somewhere, deep in the dense undergrowth, came furtive stirrings and whispers—the creatures of the night, foraging after the storm. That's all it was—but still, a sudden chill crept toward me from the darkness.

Nolan Chase had gone, and his leaving had left room for something very like elemental fear to creep back toward me. Somewhere an owl hooted, an eerily haunting call. Boze whined and I sighed, reaching down to rub his upturned muzzle.

"Okay, old guy," I told him. "Let's call it a day."

Back in the comparative coziness of the kitchen, I realized that physically I was exhausted. Yet my mind was whirling, electrically alive with restless thoughts. Too much had happened in too short a time.

I checked that darned back door again, swinging it back and forth, finally slamming it and shooting the bolt. It seemed all right. Nolan had undoubtedly been right (that was his specialty—being right, wasn't it?) and the door was just slightly out of alignment. No real problem.

I clattered the dishes into the sink, glared at the innocent-looking crack in the hearth, as if willing it to heal itself, and paced around the kitchen while the dark pressed at the windows.

My nerves were tangled with exhaustion. Nolan had convinced me that the house was secure enough. For now.

But what might be out there in the forests?

Suddenly I hated the dense, obscurant massing of trees outside and longed for the city, for the known and familiar.

Maybe I could see out over the treetops from the high tower room. The thought entered my mind as if it were an audible whisper: *Go up. Feel the freedom of the sky. Be at peace.*

The tower bay of the old house rose from the foundation through the downstairs parlor, the main bedroom on the second floor, and then up into the third-floor attics. The narrow back kitchen stairs led up, up, and up. I mounted them cautiously, Boze at my heels. Low-wattage bulbs at each landing threw our distorted shadows grotesquely along the peeled paint and plaster.

And, of course, the banister seemed loose and insecure in places, and the stairs squeaked abominably. Atmosphere.

I emerged onto the attic landing for the second time that night, pulling the chain that turned on the inadequate bulb hanging from the end of a swinging flex. Heavy boxes, trunks, castoff furniture, and clutter seemed to move within their own shadows as the light swung. A smell of long-undisturbed mustiness hung motionless in the air.

For a moment I wished that Nolan Chase was still with me. It hadn't seemed quite so—so *still* when we'd been up here together.

But then a quiet calm settled around my shoulders. Instinctively, I felt at peace. There was nothing to harm me here in this old house. It was a safe haven.

Across from the landing, toward the front of the house, were two small bedrooms; the tower room was at my right. All servants' rooms, no doubt, when the house was new. Henry Middlefield wouldn't have considered roughing it without cook and housekeeper.

That tower room. A quiet room that was home to shadows and memories. I had played here on rainy summer days in my childhood, and echoes of my own and other, earlier, children's laughter had to still be here. I wondered if the house missed that laughter.

The ceilings were lower here than on the other floors, the windows not as architecturally interesting. But through them, though they were streaked with the grime of decades, I could see the sky through breaks in the tossing branches that surrounded the house. A fat crescent of a waxing moon appeared just above the trees, caught in a tangle of chasing clouds that wisped and nearly snared themselves in the tallest pines.

Somewhere out there in that darkness were the remains of a gazebo, boathouse, and coachhouse—all being slowly reclaimed by the forest. I hadn't been out to inspect any of them yet, but their crumbling, fading silhouettes had seemed to watch me from a confusion of creepers and saplings.

A strange and nearly unfamiliar place, dimmed by shreds of childhood memories. Yet the few people I'd met in town had seemed friendly enough, even—or especially—Nolan Chase with his endless questions. He'd learned a lot more about me than I had learned about him. Well, no harm done. And surely the rest of my stay here wouldn't be nearly as dramatic as today had been. There wouldn't be any reason for Nolan or anyone else to hover over me.

Though the peace and the memories of the tower room had reassured me, I was still a little shaken. The accident on the cliffs, the power failure, the feeling that something had been at the edge of the woods—I do have a strong intuitive sense, and it was telling me that all was not well. I tried to shake off the feeling as just a reaction to the day's events.

I called Boze to me and took our shadows back down the long, steep stairs. I'd have a glass of milk and get to bed.

But I heard the phone before I reached the bottom of the kitchen flight. It startled me, insistent and unnaturally loud. I hurried to snatch it up, to cut off its intrusive shrill.

"Is the electricity still on?"

It was Nolan's voice, surprising me a little. "Yes, of course," I answered. "Everything's fine."

"I thought I'd better be sure—we just lost power on this side of town. I was—worried."

"Well, don't be. Even if the power does go out, I have the lamps and candles. You've done all you can." I wanted to add that I wasn't entirely helpless, after all, but thought that might be rude. I bit off the words.

"Okay, then." A short pause. "You had such an emotional shock today—and then to be alone in an isolated old place—"

In spite of the vestiges of prickliness, I was touched.

"I'll do fine," I assured him.

"Keep Boze in the house."

"Yes, sir. He wouldn't have it any other way."

He chuckled briefly. "Good. And I'll be in touch tomorrow."

"Thank you."

I hung up, shaking my head and smiling slightly. I really didn't know what to think of the man. Still, after a good night's sleep, everything would look more logical.

But sleep didn't come quite as quickly as I had hoped. My traitorous mind kept going back to Nolan and those moments of nearly tangible physical longing that had taken me by surprise.

And that just wouldn't do. It wouldn't do at all.

Yet he haunted my dreams that night.

The morning sunlight striking brightly across the kitchen brought a sense of cheerful reality—cheerful, at least, compared to what I'd been feeling the night before.

And it would be even brighter and more cheerful if I washed that window. Then the impact of the sheer numbers of windows in the house—as well as their height from the ground—made me groan out loud.

They could just stay dirty. But if I were going to stay for any time at all, it would be nice to remove those dust covers and search out knickknacks and ornaments to make it seem a little more like a real home. Maybe the rooms wouldn't echo as much if I unrolled a carpet or two and opened heavy draperies and sticky windows and let the present into these past-filled rooms.

A large box of old family photos had caught my attention an hour later, and I was light-years away. The jangling of the phone seemed an alien intrusion at that point, but I supposed I'd have to answer it.

"Just making sure everything is still all right," the voice on the other end said. An unexpected prickle of pleasure made me smile.

"I'm fine, Nolan. Thank you."

"Did you get some sleep?"

"Oh, yes. Lots." I couldn't very well add that I would have slept better if he'd stayed out of my dreams.

"No problems at all after I called? The power's still on?"

"I'm fine, the power's fine, everything's fine," I said

rather idiotically. "I'm going to spend the day trying to make this place less like an Addams Family residence."

"Well, good luck." He sounded dubious. "Listen, I was thinking—would you like for me to talk with Joe Wilson and see if he has time to come out and check your fireplace— the gutters, whatever? He's the town handyman, and he's coming by today to install a new outside light at the clinic. It would be a good idea if I told him that you need some help out there."

"You think I need help around here? Really? What a strange thought! The answer is yes. Definitely yes. If he has the time and inclination to help an outlander—"

"Outlander." He seemed to consider the word. "Hmmmm. He'll be there, definitely. Maybe not today, but—"

"I appreciate that. And all your help and moral support last night."

"Yes." He was silent a moment, and so was I. Then he just said, "You're welcome" in a somewhat reserved way. I heard barking in the background, and he added, "One of my patients just came in. I'll be in touch."

"Thanks again," I said, but I was talking to a dead connection. I frowned at the phone, feeling as if he'd turned his back on me in the middle of a conversation.

Peculiar man. I really shouldn't find someone like him even faintly attractive.

I went back to sorting through pictures, sweeping cobwebs out of corners, letting the sun shine in. It was mid-afternoon by the time I sneezed my way out of a closet where I'd found a wonderful stash of old linens. By then I was deeply absorbed by the fascinating tapestry of years of faded treasures and threads of family memories. I'd forgotten—temporarily—all about the need for a handyman. Or a squad of them, as the case seemed to be.

It was brought back to me when I decided to take Boze for a walk before dark, thinking I'd check out the old gazebo.

We got only as far as the broad front porch steps before I heard an approaching car engine. Nolan's van. Boze barked a greeting, but I took a step backward, feeling frowsy and dusty and unready for company of any kind.

He got out of the car, yanking a toolbox after him.

"Were you about to leave?"

I found my voice. "Not really. Just—walking the dog."

He looked at me assessingly, and I was sure every speck of dust glowed neon. "I wouldn't want to keep you. But that last step—there's a board loose. I noticed it last night. We don't need Joe Wilson for that. I had a little time and thought I'd pound it back into place. If you stepped on it wrong, you could break an ankle—and that just might be very inconvenient, since you're out on the edge of town. Not to mention painful."

"I'd just dial 911."

He snorted. "In Caribou Bay?"

But they must have some kind of county emergency system—Well, he was probably right—as usual. I could almost hear the echo of his final words the night before: *city woman.*

He transferred his attention to the step, to my relief, and pulled a hammer from his toolbox and picked up nails from the top tray. The board tipped creakingly under his hands— strong hands that quickly drove four nails firmly in before he looked up again.

"That should do it. And Joe will be out in the next few days to check out the more difficult jobs, if you'd like."

"I'd like." I hesitated momentarily. "Boze and I were going to check out the gazebo, if it's still there under all that overgrowth. Would you like to join us?'' Polite. Cool. Just the right touch of distance, I hoped.

It was his turn to hesitate. And politely, coolly, with just a touch of distance, he glanced at his watch and then nodded. ''I have to be back at the clinic by six. A man from back around Rice Flats is bringing in his dog—got mauled by a wolf, looks like.'' I must have looked startled, because he smiled slightly. ''Yes, there are still a few wolves around, but don't worry. They don't like people any better than people like them. And I'm the only vet in fifty miles or so. Where is this gazebo of yours?''

I led him through the thigh-deep thickets of grass and shrubs. He held back straggling branches, warned of poison ivy, and stopped me gently with a touch on the shoulder as a brace of pheasant clattered clumsily into the air ahead of us.

We stood close, motionless, and silence returned before he withdrew his hand from my shoulder. My heart was beating warmly in my throat, and his voice was a few notes lower when he spoke.

''I think I see the gazebo. Straight ahead—is that it?''

Through a break in the trees, a corner of the structure poked from the graceful embrace of birches—a broken ghost of its once-proud self. I sighed as I looked at it: the forest had reclaimed it, the gingerbread and railings were crumbling, creepers and shrubs almost hid it from view. A sense of sadness and loss tugged at my heart.

Boze ran ahead to check it out around the edges and dismissed it as uninteresting except for a squirrel that scampered atop the sagging roof before he could pursue it.

''Must have been pretty elegant once,'' Nolan said as if he'd tuned in to my thoughts.

''It was. I have old photos.'' My voice was a little uneven.

''I'd like to see them sometime.''

"Yes." It was a meaningless word; he was just being polite.

But he wasn't cool and distant. I could feel his warmth, so close to me in the near-jungle claiming the old gazebo. He was watching me again. I could feel the intensity of his gaze but couldn't look into his eyes.

Then his arm was around my shoulders, consoling and yet more than that. "Meg?" he asked quietly. I sensed a thousand unasked questions in that one word.

Boze broke into a frenzy of barking at some unseen small animal, breaking the spell. I managed to step out of the circle of that spell and smile—maybe a little crookedly— up at Nolan. "It feels—very lonely out here, doesn't it?" I asked, to fill the silence between us. "Very far from people. From reality. From civilization."

There was a subtle change in Nolan's eyes, in his whole attitude. "Does it?" he asked indifferently. "Well, I suppose it does, if you're used to fast lanes and city life." He looked down at his watch. "I have to get back."

"Yes," I said again, wondering at the unexpected wave of emptiness that I felt. What had I said to offend him? I turned, starting back toward the house, trying not to let him see my puzzlement—and slightly injured pride. Nolan was still close behind me, but it was as if a steel door had clanged shut between us. The magic had gone—so quickly.

And why? Darn him, he seemed to have a split personality! For a crazy moment I wanted to shake him—or both of him, as the case might be—and ask him if he couldn't just relax enough to be a friend—but no. Instinctively, on a deep level, I knew that it would be impossible to be "just a friend" to this man.

Boze whined suddenly, pressing close to my side with ears and eyes alert and head high. I wasn't sure if he was trying to protect me or himself—and from what? Was something invisible watching us from the dark depths behind the shifting patterns of the leaves? Or was Boze just sensing my mood? I glanced back at Nolan, but he just gave me a half smile, never breaking stride. Apparently he hadn't seen or felt the shiver of apprehension that had touched me and my dog.

When we reached the porch, I turned toward Nolan. "Thank you again," I said. "For all your trouble."

"It was no trouble at all." His voice was curiously flat. "Joe will take care of the really troublesome jobs." Hardly saying good-bye, he was already halfway to his van.

Boze and I stood at the top of the newly repaired steps and watched him go. Muttering to Boze about "unpredictable men," I tried to ignore—or at least soothe—my singed pride.

Boze whined again, watching the woods. I narrowed my eyes to search the darkening forest but could see nothing but shifting lights and darks caused by the fitful breeze.

Still, I hustled the dog and myself into the house and locked the doors behind me as quickly as I could. Locking out what—fears? Lost spirits from the past? The unknown?

Knowing, as I pocketed the keys, that some things simply cannot be locked out with any lock known to man. Or to woman.

Chapter Three

Over the next few days, I explored the house, trying to keep the thoughts of Doris Taylor's death from my mind. And trying, too, not to think about Nolan Chase.

Neither was easy.

Going into town and talking to people—reliving those moments on the shore—didn't appeal to me. So I stayed close to The Birches. I let decades of darkness out of closets and wondered if every box I opened might be Pandora's. I had a sneaky suspicion that just coming up here had opened a Pandora's box.

If I had come up here for a change, I was certainly getting it. But if I was supposed to be resting and regaining my equilibrium, I wasn't succeeding. . . .

On the third day I decided to investigate the attics more carefully.

Boze trailed dutifully at my heels, checking corners and old trunks and deciding there was nothing interesting here. He collapsed beside an ancient dress form and watched me sleepily.

There was something—well, a little unnerving about the shadowy attics today. The floors creaked more than I'd remembered, and there was a spot where the floorboards were loose. One edge was sticking up dangerously, and I could almost see movement out of the corner of my eye—

There *was* movement. A small squirrel, who gave me a look of dismayed surprise and then whisked away through a small hole in the roofline beside the tiny window.

Well. Another set of repairs—the floor and the window. I'd found a good many things for that marvelous handyman Nolan had mentioned.

Where was that handyman, anyway? Where, for that matter, was Nolan? Shouldn't he, in common decency, have called to see how I was getting along, rattling around alone in this creaky old place with the memory of Doris Taylor's fall still fresh in my mind?

Not that I couldn't handle it on my own, but he could at least show some concern. I'd met all kinds of men in my work and thought smugly, that I knew how to handle every type of situation. Of course, that was as an acting manager of a large hotel, not as a city woman in a small town where death had overtaken peace.

Maybe Nolan was right; maybe I didn't belong here. But that didn't give him the right to seem to reach out to me with a certain amount of compassion at one moment and tell me what a metropolitan idiot I was at the next.

He may not have said it in so many words, but that was what it came to.

Maybe he thought that if he didn't send the handyman out, I'd give up and go back to the city. That was probably an unworthy thought, but if it happened to be true—well, I was tougher than he thought.

With a touch of righteous indignation, I called Boze and headed for the stairs, arms full of a wonderful assortment of old jigsaw puzzles, mind full of the idea of calling Nolan Chase and checking once again on the name of that handyman. If he wouldn't call me, I'd call him. After all, I had a very good reason to, didn't I?

A couple of old steamer trunks caught my attention. What

was in all these boxes, trunks, old crates? I'd have to dig around in them. Something—a twinge of my sometimes unexplainable intuition—told me that I should. It was an odd feeling. The spell of the memories in this house, I told myself. Or just curiosity. I descended the stairs thoughtfully, my arms wrapped tightly around a half-dozen fragile boxes full of puzzles.

Puzzles. They were multiplying.

The voice that answered the phone at the clinic certainly wasn't Nolan's. It was silky and very feminine while managing to sound, at the same time, efficient and alert. The kind of voice I'd like my own secretary to have.

"Er—is Dr. Chase there?"

"Yes, but he's busy right now. This is Kate. Can I help you?"

"Kate?" Why should I be surprised? Shouldn't Nolan have help in the office? I wondered briefly if his help was as attractive as her voice.

"Kate Lundstrom," the voice replied patiently. "Who's calling, please?" My, she was polite.

"Meg Livingston. Out at The Birches. I—I just wanted to ask Dr. Chase a question."

"Hold on a sec. I think he's finished with this patient."

There was apparently no hold button—which was rather refreshing. Instead of canned music, I heard a murmur of voices in the background, a laugh, and then Nolan's voice, impartially friendly and questioning.

"Yes, Meg, what's up? Are you all right? Has something gone wrong?" He seemed to assume that I would automatically call *him* if something went wrong—an assumption that was probably right, darn it, since I had very few other people I knew to call on up here.

"I'm just fine," I told him. Why did he always assume

I wasn't all right? "But I wanted to get the name of that handyman. It seems I have squirrels in my attic."

There was choked laughter on the other end of the line, and I regretted my choice of words. "Really," he managed after a moment. "Does that statement mean that there are small rodents of the family sciuridae inhabiting the upper floor of The Birches?"

"Whatever," I said a little waspishly. Show-off. "Anyway, there's a hole up there, right by the eyebrow window in the roof, and heaven knows what else has taken up housekeeping in the attics—" I stopped suddenly, shivering. "Anyway, the opening should probably be closed off."

"You sound a little stressed. You're sure the isolation out there isn't getting to you? You'd really be better off in town at the lodge. They have a decent dining room, and you'd have lots of company—"

"No," I said with asperity. He was telling me what to do again. "I'm fine. The handyman?"

"Joe Wilson," Nolan said resignedly. "That's his name. I'll get in touch with him and get back to you."

"If you'll just give me his number, I can call him myself." The man seemed to think that city dwellers—particularly female city dwellers—were incapable of handling anything but taxicabs and credit cards. If that.

"He'll come out faster if I talk to him myself," Nolan said soothingly. "He's an independent old guy, but I know him pretty well. Don't worry—we'll get you taken care of."

"We." Wasn't that nice? I thanked him with extreme politeness and hung the phone up thoughtfully. What I should do, I told myself, was to think of Nolan as a sort of liaison person operating between myself and a one-man maintenance staff named Joe Wilson. It would be perfectly all right for a good liaison person to take charge in a strong, courteous, and efficient manner.

If only he weren't so darned—well, sexy was one word for it. But condescending was another, and superior a third. I'd have to watch myself. Once again I thanked my lucky stars that I had my job to go back to, just as soon as I felt up to it.

The evening was spent sorting through old photo albums and starting a jigsaw puzzle on one of the rickety card tables I'd found in a closet, waiting for the phone to ring. For Nolan to call me back. The silence was almost unbearable.

I wasn't sure I could stand all the excitement.

There was no television in the house, and the selection of radio stations was excruciating. What on earth did people do up here in the long winter evenings? Probably congregated at Red's or played bingo at the church hall. It was relaxing, all right. If it weren't for the demands The Birches made on me, I'd be half comatose by now.

The jangling of the phone jerked me out of my trance. At last—thank goodness—Nolan.

But it wasn't Nolan. It wasn't anybody. I said hello repeatedly and thought I heard a trace of breathing at the other end, then a quiet click and nothing.

A touch of fear sent tingling fingers down my backbone even as I tried to convince myself that it was just a wrong number.

When, fifteen minutes later, the phone rang again, I glared at it for a moment before I could bring myself to answer it.

But this time—

"Sorry it's late. I meant to get back to you earlier but had an emergency at the clinic. Hope I didn't wake you?"

"Of course not. All this exciting night life up here keeps

me up until all hours, anyway.'' There was even a germ of truth in that statement, what with the creaking house and mysterious depths of the forest and puzzling phone calls.

"Hmmmm," Nolan said, investing the sound with a world of disbelief. "But look at it this way—you don't have to stay forever, like some of us."

"Right," I said. "That's certainly some consolation."

"I'm sure it is. Now, in the meantime, I did get hold of Joe, and he'll be out tomorrow to look things over—maybe get a few jobs done. I think you'll like him." A brief pause. "I suppose I should have asked you if tomorrow was convenient?"

That would have been thoughtful, I told myself, but out loud I said, "It's wonderful, and thank you. I want you to know"—I took a deep breath and managed to say it, and it really was the truth, after all—"that I appreciate all your help."

"And I appreciate your appreciation." I heard a hint of a laugh under his words. "You're a very independent woman, Meg. I don't want to step on your toes. Not really."

"You don't. Not really." A suspicion stirred deep in my heart that perhaps Nolan understood me better than I'd realized. Somehow that wasn't entirely comforting. When I thanked him again and hung up, I was left with a bag of mixed emotions that I really didn't want to try to sort out.

I felt pretty sure that Nolan was attracted to me, that he'd felt that flash of awareness between us. Maybe he was just better than I was at suppressing feelings. And that was probably wise. I wouldn't be here long. No sense in getting involved, especially with a steamroller of a man. . . .

A little later I let Boze out the back door for a final run and stood on the little back porch, leaning against the posts and staring into the silent forests. No moon tonight, but the stars twinkled unbelievably close.

The trees were motionless, a huge, dark mass that loomed beyond the house. I had the odd feeling that every invisible trunk, branch, leaf, and needle was holding its breath, staring back at me, listening to my breathing.

The idea that I was being watched began to take over my mind. Impatiently, I tried to push it away. Why would anyone be standing in that tangled darkness just to watch me?

Boze, around the corner of the house, barked sharply a couple of times. I called him to me and backed through the kitchen door, not wanting to turn my back on that unknown nothingness out there. Giving the door an extra push to make sure it latched securely, I turned the key in the lock and shot the bolt.

Somewhere, just at the edge of the woods, it had looked as if one of the stars had gotten caught in the wild shrubs and vines—a sudden glint and then nothing.

I shivered even as I told myself that I was sure there was a perfectly logical explanation. It was ridiculous. Running a big hotel was a simple matter compared to trying to make sense out of the so-called "simple life" here at the Back of Beyond.

Maybe Nolan was right, after all. He seemed to think that I was out of my element, and maybe I was. I might be much better off back in Minneapolis with a property manager to handle the puzzles of The Birches.

My pride squelched that idea before it was even fully formed. I could handle it. *He* wasn't going to tell me what to do.

The next morning was bright and cool, filled with riffles and trills of birdsong. It made me feel much more cheerful.

I must be objective. While the grounds of The Birches were badly overgrown, in this morning's sunlight the forest was just that: a forest, not a huge, dark entity watching my every move, getting ready to swallow me.

It was a day, I decided, to let my hair down. Literally. By nine-thirty I'd brushed it until it almost sparked with electricity. At the hotel I wore it in a beautifully contrived twist that I'd spent many hours perfecting.

But this was the country.

I shook my head hard and let the heavy, long hair fall in its own casual way, smiling at the reflection in the mirror. I'd slept well, for a change, and my eyes had more brilliance than they'd had for quite a while. There was color in my cheeks. Maybe I was recovering, after all.

Slipping into a threadbare pair of jeans and an old green sweater that had seen too many washes, I set out with Boze, determined to check out the dock, lakeside, and carriage house.

But the gasping rattle of what sounded like an ancient military tank stopped me at the bottom of the steps. A hulking old pickup, rather ferocious looking, was disgorging an equally hulking and ferocious-looking man in faded overalls.

Behind it, much quieter, was a familiar van. Nolan was here. The driver of the pickup had to be—

"Joe Wilson," the hulk said in a voice that was surprisingly civilized. "Understand you need some help out here." He had drooping gray moustaches, a stained slouch hat that looked as if it dated from the Civil War, and eyes that twinkled.

I knew instinctively that, as a liaison person, Nolan had done very well indeed. "I certainly do," I told Joe Wilson. "I appreciate your coming out." I turned to Nolan with a five-hundred-watt smile to tell him thank you, but the smile faded to a feeble candlepower very quickly.

He was standing there, leaning against his van, looking

at me in the strangest way—checking me out slowly from head to toe, as if I were some kind of offbeat specie of wild animal that had been brought to him for identification.

And yet—not quite like that. His look both pleased and confused me. Was it approval? Something about the expression in his eyes caused a flowering of warmth to flow, unexpected and uncheckable, throughout my whole body.

Head to toe. I managed to look down quickly to make sure my jeans weren't threadbare in embarrassing places. Fighting the urge to back away, I tried a simple "Good morning." Even those two words sounded uncertain, not at all like my usual voice.

"Yeah," he said. "It is. And you look much better this morning. You look—" He shrugged and turned his gaze toward Joe Wilson, giving me a chance to fight off the effect he'd had on me. "I suppose," he said authoritatively, "that the broken gutter's one of the more important things. And that hole in the attic. Should check out the chimneys and fireplaces, too, but we can't do everything in one day."

Something clicked in my mind, a little switch that lit up a bright-red sign that said HOLD IT. That same switch killed the flood of warmth I'd felt a moment before.

"Although I certainly appreciate your help," I told him sweetly, "I'm quite aware of what needs to be taken care of around here and am capable of explaining all my needs in a clear and understandable manner."

Nolan studied me silently for a moment. Joe Wilson seemed to be trying not to laugh.

"*Are* you, now?" He had a look on his face that I interpreted as superior amusement, and I wished I'd phrased my statement just a bit differently; I must have sounded pretty self-important.

Then he gave me a half smile that had the faintest hint of apology in it. "I didn't mean to take the reins from your capable hands, Miss Livingston,'' he said with exaggerated courtesy. I half expected him to bow stiffly from the waist. ''But lining up what needs to be done can help prevent chaos. Or anarchy.''

''The benevolent dictator,'' I murmured with a touch of sarcasm.

''I can think of worse things to be called,'' he said consideringly. ''All right, then—*you* tell him. I'm sure you can handle it quite nicely.''

''Ummm,'' I managed. ''Well, the broken gutter, of course—and, yes, that hole in the attic. And there does seem to be some problem with the fireplaces and chimneys.'' I was simply repeating what Nolan had already said, and I felt a little silly. And I had an exasperated feeling that was exactly how he wanted me to feel.

In spite of myself, I smiled. It was a ridiculous situation. ''And, of course,'' I added quickly, feeling inspired, ''there will probably be repair work on some of the stairs—and there's a window upstairs loose in its frame. I'd like to get the place fairly well weatherproofed before I go back to Minneapolis.''

Joe gave me a wide grin. ''Lady,'' he said, ''you don't need a handyman. You need a construction company.''

He was right. I looked from him to Nolan and backed off a little. ''Well, since I'm not planning on staying indefinitely, just do whatever seems to be most important.''

''Whatever it needs to make it safe,'' Nolan put in. He ran his fingers through his thick mane of dark hair and stared, wooden-faced, at a point somewhere beyond my left shoulder. ''She won't be staying here forever, after all, as she so clearly points out. I don't think she likes the solitude out here in the wilderness, and there's a large hotel back in Minneapolis that can't get along without her.''

I felt as if I'd been put properly in my place. He was

doing it again—making me feel as if I didn't belong here. He might be right, but I didn't like being reminded of it at every turn.

Why did he keep reaching out with hints of warmth—and then clanging some kind of impenetrable door shut? Was it him, or was it me? It had to be him.

But then maybe I was asking for it, with my instinctive—and maybe misguided—reactions to being told by some macho male just what to do. Or were they overreactions, automatically clicking in because I was so aware of the masculine strength of him, and found it nearly irresistible on some basic level?

I'd have to think about that—but not right now.

"You are absolutely right, as usual," I said sweetly. "And I can't wait to get back to the city and out of these woods. I don't suppose you'd want a cup of coffee. You must be very busy today, with all of the creatures that want and need your attention and strong, guiding hand."

Joe Wilson leaned back against his truck, pushing his floppy hat back on his head and watching us with open amusement. "Why don't you two call it a draw, for now?" he suggested. "As for me, *I'd* like some of that coffee."

Less than an hour later Joe—with Nolan's help—had replaced the section of broken gutter and was filling the cracks in the fire wall in the kitchen fireplace with some kind of cure-all compound. He seemed to know exactly what to do, without either Nolan or I making suggestions, thank you very much.

"I'd like to go out and check the old boat dock," I told Nolan. "Not that it I'd want to rebuild it at this point. But it was a favorite spot of mine when I was about five."

"It was a great spot." Nolan saw my surprise that he knew that. "Let's go look. I used to come down here to fish once in a while when I was a kid. Your grandparents didn't mind. . . . ''

Once, there had been a long sweep of meadowlike lawn that led to the lake. Now it was brambly, uneven. I could see, even from a distance, that portions of the dock and pier were slanting and gradually slipping into the chilly waters of Lake Birchleaf.

"There used to be a platform out at the end," I said wistfully, remembering some of the old photos that I'd unearthed. "I think that years ago the original Middlefields had genteel picnic luncheons under umbrellas out there on fine days."

"Half of it's still there. The railings are pretty rotted." We walked out along the damp, mossy dock, carefully watching for broken boards. Under us, the water lapped gently at the old pilings, and it seemed to me that if I half closed my eyes I'd still see the garden hats and parasols clustered at the end of the dock and hear a fugitive hint of laughter from long ago.

"Watch it," Nolan warned, pulling me back from a break in the decking. "It's slippery—dangerous."

He was just a second too late. A gull swooped toward me, and I sidestepped quickly—and unwisely. My foot slipped from a slanted board, and my head hit a railing. The sudden impenetrable nothingness couldn't have lasted for more than a few seconds, a minute at the most. Dawning awareness, a return to reality was bittersweet: a confusion of the ebbing of the shock and the consolation of strong arms gripping me.

I had collapsed in a boneless heap on the dock, and Nolan was kneeling beside me, holding me against his shoulder with a strong tenderness I'd never have suspected in him.

Boze was whining, trying to lick my face and help me back to my senses. I felt Nolan push him gently away with one hand, and the dog obediently fell silent. Nolan apparently sensed my stirring consciousness and drew his head back to look at me, but didn't release his hold.

And I didn't want him to. I buried my face against his shoulder and breathed deeply—the scent of tweedy wool, faint woodsmoke, a hint of soap—

"Take it easy. You're going to have a bruise on your forehead, I'm afraid."

"Just give me a minute—" How could I have been so clumsy? I took a deep breath, allowing my head to stay securely against his shoulder while my fingertips gingerly explored a tender area already beginning to swell near my temple.

"Felled by a sea gull," I said disgustedly.

He smiled and reached out to touch the bump on my forehead with light fingers. Then he bent his head to leave a butterfly kiss on the spot.

I don't know which of us was the most surprised that he'd done that. "To help make it well," he muttered, leaning away from me and staring out across the water.

"Well," I said. "And do you do that with all your patients? Is that the secret of your success?"

"Only the ones I think are reasonably tame," he answered, and there was reluctant laughter in his voice. "I probably shouldn't have done it this time." After a moment he said, "Sorry."

"Don't be," I told him. "It feels better already."

"I'm glad." He was still studiously not looking at me directly. "I'll help you get back to the house, then. Joe should be done by now, and you should have a cup of tea and a rest."

"I can get myself back up to the house," I said a little crossly—partly because he was taking charge again, partly because my feelings were a little hurt at the way he'd pulled back, become so impersonal. "Thank you. I'm sure I'm stronger than you think I am."

He looked thoughtful, then shrugged. "Whatever. Just trying to be helpful." He called Boze back from his run along the shore, and we turned and walked back up the slope with a careful two feet of distance between us. My head throbbed with every step, and I could have done with a bit of support and encouragement.

But I certainly wasn't going to admit that.

Joe was just about finished. He straightened from his work to cluck at the bump on my head and hear what had happened. "Have to be careful around these old places," he said. "Just never know what's going to happen next." He wouldn't bother to fill the cracks in the hearth in the kitchen, he said; they were cosmetic, no real problem, and it might be as well just to leave them alone.

"Might build a fire tonight, though," he suggested, clamping his disreputable old hat back on his head and taking the check I handed him with an appreciative smile. "The heat'll help to set that compound and make it stronger. And it'll be a good night for the warmth of a fire." He looked from Nolan back to me with an innocent expression. "You can sure feel the chill in the air this afternoon, can't you?"

Oh, couldn't you, though? I glanced sideways at Nolan's unreadable face and decided that a fire in the fireplace would be wonderful. Joe promised to come back in a day or so to check the banister railings. Nolan told me, predictably and not looking directly at me, to try to be careful, and they were gone.

I rubbed vigorously at my arms, but the chill remained.

Chapter Four

He stood at the far side of a clearing, and behind him, half lost in the shadows, stood a woman whose face seemed indistinctly familiar to me.

There were things I wanted to know—things I had to know—but when I tried to cross the clearing, to draw closer, unseen roots snared my feet, and invisible force waves pushed against me like a strong wind.

"Nolan!" I screamed—but the scream was only a thin keening, a brittle nothingness. "Why are you pushing me away? Who is with you?"

Hands on hips and feet apart, Nolan stared, seemed to be seeing right through me. He turned, as if in slow motion, and looked behind him. "There's no one there, Meg. No one. You're imagining things again, Meg. You need to rest, Meg. You need to get well, so you can go back to the city. Do you need another kiss, Meg, to make it all better? I'll help you, Meg."

He was coming toward me so effortlessly—on the force of that strange, satanic wind. Suddenly I wanted to run, to escape, but I still couldn't move.

When he got to me, his arms went around me, and I felt as if I'd been gathered into the very heart of him. His kisses dissolved me, and a huge explosion left the sound of a million shards of glass settling around me—and then ashes and emptiness.

I awoke, heart pounding, tangled in the sheets and blankets. It was several minutes before my breathing and my heart rate returned to normal. Early light, blessedly normal dawn light, was sifting through the curtains. Boze had his muzzle on the side of the bed, watching me, whimpering slightly.

"It's okay, guy," I whispered to the dog, untangling the sheets and sitting on the edge of the bed. He relaxed, tail thumping the floor. He might be convinced, but I wasn't. That dream had been too real, too easy for me to understand.

It took three cups of coffee and a lot of serious talking to myself before the remnants of the dream faded, and even then, the ending of it, the emotions I'd felt, kept sweeping back over me with an intensity that was anything but dreamlike.

I tried to distract myself by working on the jigsaw puzzle I'd started. It was a 1920's Maxfield Parrish print—nude nymphs in a forest. Their woodland was full of innocence, sun, and joy. Mine seemed full of gnomes and trolls and narrowed, watching eyes.

Abandoning the puzzle, I attempted to concentrate on the report I'd have to present to the board of directors at our next meeting. It seemed to belong to another world, and my mind wouldn't stay on it. I left the papers in a heap at one side of the table and paced the house, restless.

At midmorning I stood in the tower curve of the porch, still another cup of coffee in hand, a contented Boze at my side. It was a vermilion-and-gold Indian summer day, with a sky so blue it almost hurt to look at it. Eyes closed, I lifted my face to the sunlight.

A sound made me open them again. And I found it necessary to grasp the porch railing with my free hand for support. Ahead of me, very quiet, staring up at me from the far side of the drive, stood Nolan. Almost as in my dream.

"I—I didn't hear you drive up."

"I parked back at the curve. Didn't mean to startle you. Is everything all right? What happened?"

"What do you mean, what happened? Nothing happened."

He backed off a step or two, looking up at the tower with narrowed eyes, then came toward me. "There's a window broken up on the third floor of the tower. I caught a glimpse of it as I came around the curve. You can see it pretty clearly from there."

"A window? But that can't be—"

"Come here and look if you don't believe me."

I set my coffee cup down on the railing and obediently went down the stairs toward him, wondering what he was talking about. This time, no dream roots snared my feet, and no ghosts lurked behind him.

But when I turned to look up, I saw the glass—shattered into a million pieces that glinted off the surface of the porch roof that encircled the second floor. And I remembered the end of my dream, the feeling that it had exploded around me.

"Gunshot, I think," he said. "Let's go up and have a look inside. You didn't hear it happen?"

"I—I don't know. I dreamed something—" I stopped. I couldn't begin to explain the dream. "How can you tell it's a gunshot, for heaven's sake?"

"Trust me. I know what it looks like. There are a lot of sportsmen and plinkers around here. I carry a .22 myself in the truck." He was already striding up the porch stairs, Boze happily dogging his heels, and I trailed behind him, feeling as if this, too, must be some kind of dream. "What time was it that you 'dreamed something'?"

"Just at daybreak. But why would anyone shoot at the window?"

"I don't know. It could have been an accident." He sounded doubtful and stopped on the second-floor landing to turn toward me. "Meg Livingston, do you attract trouble, by any chance?"

"I never did before, but since I got here, I'm beginning to wonder. It certainly makes life interesting, anyway." My attempt at lightness fell flat.

"If you want to call it that. I thought I'd stop by on my way home to see how your head was and find yet another minor disaster. How *is* your head, by the way?" He reached out and gently brushed the hair off my forehead with a touch so light it made me shiver.

I moved a step closer to him and then checked myself. "It's just fine. Really. It was nice of you to come by, though." I had to stop myself again. There was entirely too much warmth in my voice. "On your way home?" I asked. He'd been out early, apparently.

"I had a call before daylight—one of Carl Sander's prize goats. The goat's okay, but Carl's a nervous wreck. He worries too much, living way out in the back of nowhere with no one but goats to talk to. He's even beginning to look like an old goat."

All right, I even had to chuckle. Even though he added, just a little pointedly, "Some people can handle the solitude of the country; some can't. Carl's a city transplant. City transplants find it difficult to adjust sometimes."

"Some may," I told him. "As for me, I'm doing fine."

"Great. I suppose it may work if you're not planning on developing deep roots." He sounded skeptical. "Let's go look at that window. I can arrange to have Joe come out and fix things up and call Jack Darling.''

He was taking over again. This time I felt no resentment about that, just acceptance. He wasn't trying to be domineering; he was helping—in his own way.

But I was afraid of so much strength and self-confidence in a man I was so physically attracted to—there, I'd admitted it without even hesitating!—for the memories of my mother, her meekness and misery still wouldn't leave, would never leave.

There was more broken glass inside the room than there had been on the roof, and Nolan sharply ordered Boze to stay in the doorway. "You, too," he commanded, looking at me. I obeyed as readily as Boze did. It was a mess.

Nolan stepped into the room, scanning the wall opposite the window. "Now, if there'd been a nice, neat hole with a few cracks around it, we'd know for sure," he muttered. "But that old glass just shattered—but yeah, there it is. Above the door. Bet it was a varmint rifle, a .22.''

"Why?" I could hardly get the word out. "Why would anyone shoot at the window?"

"It could have been kids, I suppose. Out early, plinking— either bad aim or a bad idea of fun. Could be." He walked back over to me, his gaze soft. "Hey. You're as pale as a ghost.''

His sympathy brought a strained, choked laughter that was mixed with tears. Nolan put his hands on my shoulders, close to my neck, and gently massaged the tender area under my ears. My whole body trembled slightly, and then I stood still, letting the waves of warmth flood through me. For that brief moment, nothing mattered but his touch.

Nolan was the one who stepped back, dropping his hands to his side. "We'd better get downstairs and make some calls. Though I doubt if we'll ever know who did it.''

"Or why." We were on the stairs now, heading down, and I was amazed that my knees were carrying me without collapse. But I had to stop, leaning against the newel post for support, when we reached the bottom. "Oh, no," I said as an awful thought snaked its way into my mind.

"Oh, no what?" He'd turned to look at me, frowning a little.

"That's one of my favorite places to look out over the forest. What if somebody thought they saw me there, saw a shadow—but that's impossible. Who'd want to shoot me?" It was a ridiculous thought. And yet it gave me a cold feeling in the pit of my stomach. "Why?" I asked yet again. There was no answer this time, either.

"I don't think that's what happened, Meg. But I like the idea of your staying alone out here less and less as time goes by." The shutters had come down behind his eyes again. "Go back to the city, Meg. Or at least move to the lodge in town."

"No. I'm staying here."

"Stubborn woman. Obviously you won't listen to reason."

I started to object that I was eminently reasonable under reasonable circumstances, but he went on. "I'll make those calls, then. And get on back to town. . . . ."

While he called, I sat down and made a great show out of shuffling my stacks of papers, pretending to study my report to the board. *I could have called them myself,* I told myself, trying to summon up the resentment I would have felt a few days earlier if Nolan had taken over. But it was all right for now. In fact, some secret corner of my psyche was appreciating all that vibrant strength of his, though I tried to ignore that. And, after all, he wouldn't be running my life forever.

"Jack will make a report, and Joe will be out this after-noon late," Nolan told me when he hung up.

I looked up at him, managed a polite thank you and a smile, and stacked my papers neatly.

He leaned against the wall, watching me silently for a moment. "Homework?" he asked at last.

"A report to the board," I told him. "Due next month.
. . ."

"Your job must be very important. And difficult."

"Yes and no," I told him. "I love it. It's been hard work and a lot of schooling and apprenticeship time, and now—well, I'm in line for the top job."

"Congratulations," he said a little dryly. "Must be a glamorous line of work. Meeting all those interesting peo-ple, doing exciting things—"

"And," I reminded him, "working very hard. Plus com-peting against the old-boy network that has always run the show." I stopped myself. None of this could be of any interest to him.

"Mmmmmm." He was watching me coolly, and it was as if the current that had been between us had been turned off. "Well, I do have to get back. You be careful, you hear?"

I promised him I would and went back into the house and tried to concentrate once again on that darned report. It had turned into a meaningless jumble, and I gave up in disgust.

By the next morning, the window was fixed, Joe had given his opinion that it was probably just kids who needed a good talking to, and I had managed to get a good night's sleep. If I had dreams, I didn't remember them.

But my waking mind ran in tight little circles. I couldn't

concentrate on the report. An unwelcome suspicion had nudged at a tiny window in my mind.

Nolan had been out before daybreak. And he carried a .22 in the truck, and he very much, for some reason, wanted me to get out of here and go back to the city. Why? And did he want me to go back badly enough to try to frighten me out of my senses? Ridiculous. Still, the thought wouldn't quite go away.

But it was too beautiful a morning for disturbing thoughts. Much too perfect a day to stay in the house. And I still hadn't checked out the carriage house. Maybe now would be a good time.

I called Boze and started down the path. In this vivid daylight, the forest seemed to lighten and pull back. It was darkly peaceful, though I was acutely aware of the quiet.

As if the forest were holding its breath.

I didn't quite make it to the carriage house. The remnants of the old pathway were still muddy from the recent storms, and puddles glinted amid the shifting leaf shadows.

In one of the damp areas beside the path there were footprints. They looked like a man's prints, like heavy-duty bootprints, not a boy or group of boys—and besides, it occurred to me, did boys get up at dawn just to go plinking? They weren't Joe's or Nolan's prints—neither of them had been down this path.

They led toward the carriage house, and they'd been made after the rain. I looked toward the carriage house and shivered, then fled back to the house. I'd better let Jack Darling know.

He wasn't there—he was out on an accident report three miles down the highway. No, I told the officer on duty, it wasn't an emergency. I'd speak to him later. After all, the shooting had been the day before. And it was unlikely that anyone would still be skulking around.

But I was frightened, and the coward in me refused to go back and explore the carriage house. Boze was too much of a good-natured pussycat to be much protection, so I simply hibernated, locking doors, closing windows, and wondering if I was becoming paranoid.

I tried to distract myself by working on my report—all the while cursing George Baldwin and his "old boy" mentality. He was not an easy man to work with. Thank goodness he'd be retiring in a year. It was an uncharitable thought and selfish, too—because then his position would be mine. *I* would be the woman who'd take over; the board would approve unanimously.

Wouldn't they?

I couldn't concentrate. Thoughts of Doris Taylor, shot-out windows, and mysterious bootprints made a muddle of my thinking.

And, of course, thoughts of Nolan Chase kept superimposing themselves on all the other things.

Pushing the report aside impatiently, I worked for about ten minutes on the jigsaw puzzle. Naturally, none of the pieces wanted to fit.

The ringing of the phone jolted me back to the present, to reality. I grabbed it as if it were a lifeline.

"It's Nolan. Just thought I'd check in to be sure everything's okay now. Joe got the window fixed, did he? And you aren't in any more trouble?"

I was reasonably sure he meant it in fun, but it wasn't funny, and besides—understandably—I was feeling edgy. "I'm perfectly okay. Thank you for asking, but you don't need to worry about me. I'm used to taking care of myself."

"Mmmmm. If you say so. Still, I was thinking—you'd better stay off that dock. It's definitely spongy, isn't safe."

"I'd already figured that out." I told myself that it was reassuring that he was so concerned about my safety and at the same time wondered why he had to make it sound as if he were giving me an ultimatum. Yet, darn, I cared that he cared enough to do so. This wasn't part of the script, and I didn't know my lines. "It could be dangerous out there, I know," I tried.

But that just brought the memory of the feel of his arms around me, of the tentative healing kiss, and my voice faltered as a warmth like the sun on an Indian summer day swept over me, silencing rational thought.

"Yes, it can, can't it?" He paused. Were we thinking of the same thing? "I just want you to be safe."

"I understand. So do I. Believe me." Should I mention the footprints? But that would no doubt bring on another flood of advice and directions, and I wasn't sure I could handle that.

I didn't have to mention the footprints to bring it on. There was another short silence. "Meg," he said at last, "you probably don't want to hear this, but I do feel you should leave The Birches. Go back to Minneapolis, or take a cruise, or at the very least check in at the lodge here in town for a few days."

The authoritative note was back in his voice. "I'm staying here. I have things to take care of."

"Meg, you're just being stubborn."

"Yes, I am. And I'm staying," I told him and could hear the tiny edge of defensive anger in my voice. Overreaction? He'd said he just wanted me to be safe, but what he really wanted to do was to run my life for me. I knew how to handle people like that—as long as I didn't find them so darned attractive.

That faint suspicion that he could have been the one to shoot out the window crept back into my mind. I tried to dismiss it as mean-spirited and unworthy. He couldn't . . . he wouldn't . . .

"I'm sure you're very capable," he started, but I cut in.

"Look, I can work things out," I told him. "If I need help, I'll certainly let you know."

A few more cool, short sentences, and our conversation was over. I wasn't very happy—with myself or with him.

I had to escape for a while. Minutes later I was dashing cold water over my face, slipping into black tights and an oversized blue sweater, pulling my hair back into a ponytail and sweeping concealing bangs across the bump on my forehead. I'd go into town and check on my mail, stop for coffee at Red's, and involve myself somehow in the living, breathing life of the town.

I left Boze in the kitchen and hoped he'd at least have the good sense to bark if anyone came near the house; he didn't look happy at the idea of staying alone. I couldn't blame him.

Grabbing my car keys, I fled the whispering uncertainties of the old house and headed, with a sense of relief, to Caribou Bay.

I picked up my mail and didn't like it much. There was a letter from George Baldwin that I read twice before pulling away from the post office muttering a few choice words.

Coffee and a sandwich and time to think, that's what I needed. A few minutes later I was seated in a booth at Red's, and Edina was standing beside me, a stout pillar of reassurance.

"Why, Miss Livingston. You do look better today. Nolan got you home okay, did he? Nice man, Nolan, isn't he?"

I couldn't disagree, but had she put a shade of meaning into the question? "Nice, yes. Please call me Meg. And do I ever need a cup of coffee!"

"Good and strong, yah. And a smoked turkey breast

sandwich, I'll bet, and that sweater does match your eyes, doesn't it? You do look pretty today.''

That made me feel better, that and the coffee she brought a few minutes later. ''Nolan and Joe helping you out with some repair work, are they?''

Nothing was secret in a small town. That I knew. ''Thanks. Yes. Nolan's very good at taking charge of things.''

She either didn't hear the touch of sarcasm in my voice or chose to ignore it. ''Mmmmm. Needs someone to take care of, he does. Besides his animals, I mean. He's been alone too much, ever since Chrissie—'' She broke off, biting at her bottom lip as if she'd said too much. But there was a tiny gleam in her eye that made me think she knew exactly what she was saying and why.

''Chrissie?'' I prompted, my heart doing a funny little flip.

''He was married once, six years back or so, but that's his story, not mine to tell, isn't it?'' Now, her expression said, *I've planted the seed, and it's up to you to go on from there.*

I didn't dare ask any more questions—they were running through my head like a swarm of bees.

So. I'd just have to find out more about Nolan's past. Not that it really mattered, in the long run, but it might help me understand what made him tick. And I probably wasn't going to be able to avoid him completely during my stay. What's more, I wasn't sure that I *wanted* to.

A strange prickling sensation interrupted my thoughts— an uncomfortably familiar feeling. I was being watched. I turned my head slowly and discovered that Judd Patterson was sitting at a table halfway across the floor. The cheerful smile he gave me chased away the traces of uneasiness.

"Hi. All alone? Mind if I join you? I've been thinking about you, hoping you'd recovered from the shock."

Nice, up-front, uncomplicated approach. I smiled back at him. Maybe his easy company would help chase away the goblins and gremlins that kept haunting my thoughts.

He slipped into the booth across from me, his eyes sweeping over me appreciatively. "You look great. Getting everything under control out there at the old place? Must be quite a job. I admire you for tackling it."

Not only nice, but approving. No hidden antagonism, no unasked-for advice. Maybe a touch smooth and ingratiating, but I'd handled that type at the hotel—in several languages. It was an easy type to handle, compared to some others. Like Nolan.

"I won't get everything taken care of before winter, I'm afraid," I told Judd. "But at least it'll be a little more secure against the weather—against intruders."

"Don't tell me you've had someone breaking in."

"Not—not that I know of." But those footprints—and the feeling of eyes watching from the forest. . . .

My expression must have changed at those thoughts, because he regarded me with a curious expression. "Well," he offered at last, "I guess it might be kind of nerve-wracking, being all alone out there. Maybe you should have brought a friend with you."

"I have my dog. And, in a way, I enjoy the peace and quiet."

"Hmmmm." This from behind me, one of Nolan's "hmmmmms," this time full of amusement and disbelief. "When you can get it. Mind if I sit down?" As if we'd never exchanged those cool words on the phone a little while before. . . .

There was no polite way to say no, and I didn't want to say no, and besides, he had already slipped in beside me.

Carefully, I thought, so that he wouldn't be too close—yet I could feel that magnetic warmth, even over the intervening space between us. It managed to find its way through the cool barrier he'd built around himself whenever he was around me.

The bee swarm of questions about Chrissie immediately buzzed back into my head, but this was certainly no time to ask them. "I *do* enjoy the peace and quiet," I said a little crossly. "When I can get it. That's what I came up here for, after all."

Judd chuckled. "Me, too," he said, "that and the changing colors and the clean air. But then I didn't witness a violent death, and I'm not stuck out in the woods alone in a haunted house."

Nolan stirred, moving an inch closer to me. I don't think he even knew he did it.

Haunted house, indeed. "What do you do—when you're not leaf creeping and breathing clean air?" I asked Judd.

"I'm a systems analyst. Out of Kansas City, actually—though I travel a lot."

"Sounds pretty interesting." Nolan was gazing at Judd assessingly, and it wasn't hard to tell that he didn't find the career of traveling systems analyst pretty interesting at all.

A slight suspicion—or was it a hope?—that Nolan might just be a bit jealous fluttered momentarily at the edges of my thoughts and then disappeared. Why should he be?

And what had Chrissie been like?

I pushed that stubborn thought from my mind and realized that Judd was asking me something that I caught just the tail end of. "—thought about selling the old place?"

"It's a possibility," I admitted, gazing down at my lukewarm coffee.

On cue, Edina materialized behind us with a fresh pot,

and conversation lagged for a moment as she refilled the cups. She was concealing a knowing smile, I could swear.

"But not right now," I went on. "Probably not, anyway. It's been in the family for so long. . . . "

"Well, there might be a possibility I'd be interested." It was so unexpected that I looked at Judd with a touch of shock.

"You can't be serious. What on earth would you do with it?"

"I have friends, acquaintances, clients who are hunters and fishermen. I might be able to turn it into a lodge."

I hardly had time to turn the idea over in my head before Nolan was speaking—and in a very definite voice.

"Meg isn't really interested in selling at this point, but it's certainly something to keep in mind."

I was on the verge of telling him that I could speak for myself, thanks so much, when I got my first glimpse of Kitty.

Red had appeared behind the bar, his young bobcat friend lopped in a relaxed way across his shoulders. It really was an electrifying sight—the cat was nearly full grown, and its deceptively drowsy appearance masked an inherent wildness that even a city woman like myself couldn't miss.

"Nice Kitty," I murmured. Red beamed proudly.

"Like her?" Nolan asked with a touch of amusement.

"Well, from a distance. I wouldn't get too close, too soon."

I'm sure it was unconscious, but he moved an inch away from me again. "Like people. Have to get to know them." He looked at Red. "You know, Red, your insurance carrier's going to catch you toting Kitty around one of these days. If she took a swipe at a customer it'd be trouble."

Red looked indignant. "Naw, Nolan. I worry about what

the customers might do to my Kitty. I keep her away from them.''

"Look at the size of those feet!" Judd was staring in fascination at the cat, with a very wary look, for which I didn't blame him. Kitty wasn't a scratch-behind-the-ears cat.

"Easy to track," Nolan said, amused. "Besides, she keeps her claws in when she's around Red."

"You haven't clipped her claws?" Judd asked in disbelief.

"You're yoshing me, yah? She has to climb, don't she? She has her big pen out back, and trees, and a treehouse. But no staircase, see?"

"I suppose." Judd and Kitty seemed to be involved in a staredown, and Kitty was grumbling a bit deep in her throat, flexing her big paws.

"She'd leave huge footprints," I said idly, then said "Oh" as I remembered.

Nolan looked at me sharply. "Oh, what?"

"Footprints. I found some near the carriage house—big prints in the mud. Someone's been prowling out there, I think."

"You've seen someone prowling around The Birches?" Judd asked, leaning forward a little.

"No, I haven't seen anyone. I just have this feeling— Anyway, the prints probably weren't important."

"Good heavens, Meg, why didn't you say something before? After having the window shot out like that—" There was an edge to Nolan's voice that I hoped was concern and not anger.

"A window shot out?" Judd sounded disbelieving. "But why? Was it kids? Vandalism?"

"We don't know," Nolan answered abruptly. "But we'd like to find out. Come on, Meg. Let's go back to the house and take a look. Now." He glanced quickly at me, as if waiting for an explosion.

But this time I was actually grateful for his steamroller approach. Common sense beat down pride. For the moment. "Right," I said, grabbing my bag and fishing out money to cover my sandwich and coffee. "Good idea. Thank you."

Nolan looked pleased and surprised at my reaction, but shook his head when Judd offered to come along. "Not a good idea, thanks," he said. "The more there are of us, the more chance of obliterating prints."

Rebuffed, Judd subsided reluctantly. "Okay. I get the picture. Good luck. And, Meg—be careful." He gave me a small, sympathetic smile for which I was grateful.

His feelings apparently weren't easily hurt. I looked back over my shoulder at him as we left. He grinned and threw me a kiss—it was so unexpected that I chuckled and threw one back.

I turned back to see Nolan holding the door for me, an impatient frown pulling his brows together. Well, he was kind, too, in his own domineering way. And once again I thought I detected just an edge of jealousy.

Was it just wishful thinking? And if it was real, should I be pleased, or amused, or wary? Judd's words echoed in my mind: *Good luck. And, Meg—be careful.*

Chapter Five

Nolan followed close behind me on the drive back to
The Birches. It was reassuring to have him so near.

Of course I could have handled all of this on my own.
Of course I could. I could have talked to Jack Darling and
somehow dealt with trespassers and squelched all those uneasy feelings.

But it *was* reassuring to have Nolan near. I hadn't forgotten the sharp words we'd exchanged, but, after all, there
were times when differences should be put aside. And this
was one of those times.

Boze heard us drive up to the front porch and created an
enormous ruckus before I could even get up the front steps
to unlock the door and deposit my bag and my mail in the
house. Nolan was right on my heels, slipping through the
door behind me as close as my shadow.

"Does he always bark like that when you come home?"

I caught the question behind the question. "Sometimes,"
I said. "He does get excited about nothing. Actually, I think
he's barking because he hears you with me." I called out
to Boze to be quiet, and he subsided into a few excited,
strangled whimpers.

"See?" I asked smugly. It would be ridiculous to think
that anyone had tried to come in when I wasn't there—that

there was an intruder, that Boze was barking at something—
at someone—besides us.

"Mmmmmm," Nolan said noncommittally. But we
checked the dark corners on our way to the kitchen, just to
be sure. At least *I* did, wondering if I was slightly paranoid,
though I was pretty sure Nolan was being watchful, too.
And Boze's wagging tail and whoofles of joy when we
opened the door to the kitchen dispelled any doubts either
of us might have had.

"You see," I said with a touch of relief, "he's just so
glad to see us, that's all." Boze went immediately to Nolan,
fawning around his feet in a happy frenzy. "For some reason, he seems to adore you."

I suppose I sounded slightly miffed at being ignored by
my own dog, because Nolan gave me a funny grin. "Hard
to believe, isn't it? But most dumb animals do. Dogs included." He rubbed the top of Boze's head and accepted
with equanimity the enthusiastic hand-licking he got in return. "Now, where were these mysterious footprints?"

"Along the path to the carriage house," I answered.
"And Boze isn't dumb."

"Doggie-dumb and people-dumb are two different
things," Nolan assured me, as if I didn't know. "Smart as
he is, though, he's not going out to the carriage house with
us. With those big feet, he'd probably romp all over any
other footprints."

"I honestly don't know what you think you're going to
find, or what you could possibly tell from anything you
might find, when you get right down to it."

"When you get right down to it, I'm hoping to be able
to tell—possibly—which direction those footprints came
from and which way they went. That might help. I am not
Sherlock Holmes. I'm not going to tell you that the man

smoked cheroots and worked on a fishing boat and wore a Dodgers baseball cap. But I *am* a pretty good tracker.''

''Lot of good that's going to do us. Even if you're a bloodhound at heart.'' If I sounded a little sarcastic, it was probably because he sounded so darned superior. Again. Sometimes putting differences aside was no easy task.

''Maybe.'' He looked at me with a touch of amusement. ''But you don't grow up in these parts without learning something of tracking—not if you have any interest at all in the outdoors. And I always did.''

I glanced up at him as we let ourselves out the back door, leaving a disappointed dog to sulk in the kitchen. The noon-time shadows played across Nolan's face in a way that brought a strong suspicion to my mind.

Somewhere, generations back, there could have been— probably had been—an infusion of Native American blood into the Chase line. Now that I saw it, I wondered that I had missed it before. Algonquin, Chippewa, perhaps— someday I'd ask him about it. If I stayed around here long enough to really get to know this man.

''Go slowly,'' he instructed, breaking in on my thoughts. ''Let me know fifteen feet ahead of time, if you can.''

''I can. It was just beyond the clump of sumac. There. At the bend of the path.''

''Hmmmmm.'' He stopped, putting one hand on my shoulder, standing very still for a moment. Suddenly all of my senses were sharpened: the warmth and pressure of that hand, the slight stirring of the breezes in the branches above us. The whirring rasp of a katydid or locust somewhere nearby, a bird chirruping a few feet away, the resinous aroma of the towering pines.

But most of all, I was aware of the hand on my shoulder. Its warmth seemed to radiate through me, to root me to the spot.

And then he slowly removed his hand and turned from me, scanning the weeds and grasses at the side of the path. Reality clicked back in. Odd how reality seemed to create a hollow cold spot somewhere deep inside.

This wasn't like me. I tried to shake myself out of the sense of disappointment, but it hung stubbornly about me like ancient cobwebs.

"Mmmmhmmm." He was squatting now beside the path, visually measuring and cataloging every blade of grass and shrub branch within ten feet. "Came through here, I think." He looked up at me. "Did you go off the path at all along here?"

"No, I'm sure I didn't."

"Then"—he stood up and studied other branches, shoulder high—"whoever it was did come this way. From the main road, probably. You can get through that way if you know how to cross the ravine between Birch Creek and the road."

"Which means," I said thoughtfully, "that whoever it was had to be familiar with the ground?"

"Looks that way. Not a casual trespasser, anyway."

"But a trespasser."

There had to be a logical, innocent reason for someone to have come this way; I just had to use a good dose of common sense to find it. "It could have just been a hiker," I tried, not even convincing myself.

"Not too likely. There are better places to hike." He moved forward, and I followed. "He was heading for the carriage house, all right. And recently."

"Are—are we going *into* the carriage house?"

"Of course. Though I don't see any signs of which way he went when he left. Do you want to go back to the house? Could be somebody in there sleeping off a hangover."

"I want to know."

"Lead on, then, Watson. But slowly, so I can observe."

The brush crackled a few feet away, and I instinctively moved closer to Nolan. "It's all right," he said soothingly. "That was just a pair of squirrels out for a romp. I saw them a minute or two ago watching us from a tree trunk."

Well, he hadn't missed *that*, anyway. But I stayed close to Nolan, anyway—just in case. This was no time for personal nonsense like privacy zones.

Wordlessly, we reached the bottom of the exterior stairs that led to the apartment above the old stables.

"Stop," he said softly at the bottom of the steps. His hand found my shoulder again, and he moved up behind me so closely that I could feel the warmth of his body. It caused those strangely pleasant sensations to return. "There are no footprints on the steps." An ordinary enough statement, but there was a husky awareness in his voice that made me think he had experienced at least some of what I'd felt. "I suppose he could have gone in downstairs, into the stables."

"It's all one big room now, a garage." I was surprised at how normal my voice sounded. "No one could hide there." There was a window grimed with the dust of decades under the rise of the open staircase, and we moved, still close, still touching, to look in.

Nothing. Just gray dust, old cans, benches, tires—debris left from another age, all covered with cobwebs and silence. Inside, a large, lethargic fly threw itself against the cracked pane of the window again and again, buzzing in frustration.

"Upstairs, then? Step carefully—some of the boards look treacherous."

He dropped his hand and moved away toward the steps, but that charged atmosphere between us remained, almost as if it were alive. He went first on the stairs, testing the way. I followed in silence, beginning to wonder if all of this was some mental aberration on my part—a short-circuiting of brain waves, that made me feel attracted to a man who could never be part of my life. I almost hoped that it *was* something like that.

But at the top of the stairs, that hope was exploded when Nolan turned and looked into my eyes with an intensity that almost burned through me. I knew then he was sensing—and sharing—my feelings, and I had to look away from him before I lost whatever shred of common sense I might have left.

"What are you thinking, Meg?" A direct challenge.

Oh, I wished he hadn't asked that. "That—that maybe someone's inside up here." I tried, nearly inaudibly. "Come on, we've got to check it out. We can't let this place spook us."

Nolan took a deep breath and turned from me, apparently seeking his own level of normalcy. "So who's spooked? Let's get inside, make sure everything's okay. The upper floor was an apartment, wasn't it?"

His attempt at a logical question helped bring us both back to normal. "Yes. For the groom, or chauffeur, I suppose. Probably abandoned a long time ago. Oh—I didn't think to bring the big ring of house keys, and I suppose the door's locked."

"No, Meg, it isn't." His hand was on the dull brass doorknob now, and the doorknob—and then the door—protestingly moved as he put some pressure on them.

We slipped inside, still so close together that we moved almost as one, and stood motionless in the small amount of dusty light that the partially open door reluctantly allowed into the room.

I thought I heard something, a scrabbling off to the left, but the sound stopped before I could be sure. Very little light penetrated the dirt-hazed windows, and even that little was further cut off by large boards which leaned against them.

"You stay here by the door. I'm going to check the other rooms."

"Not on your life," I told him. "I'm going with you. I remember the layout." Both of us were whispering, and it seemed as if the whispers echoed from the corners of the room.

A table with a broken leg tilted drunkenly against a side wall; two overstuffed, broken-springed chairs sagged near it, shreds of old upholstery disgorging gray stuffing. Everywhere, dust made everything a uniform gray.

There was something rather frightening about it, and I couldn't figure out why. But a haunting, long-buried childhood memory nearly surfaced—of one of my aunts gossiping in a low voice about poor Adelaide and the carriage house and death, and being shushed by my grandmother. I felt an intuitive chill of fear, and I caught my breath on something like a sob.

Nolan heard it and was beside me in an instant, gathering me close against him. He offered strong, solid masculine muscle and bone to which I clung, burying my face in his shoulder.

"Meg?" The gentle word was a question that came from far away and yet was as close as his breath on my ear.

Looking up at him, I started to explain that I just had a small case of the shivers—but I never had the chance.

Our lips and bodies met with a singing, indescribable hunger that consumed us both. I don't think I'd ever responded to a man in quite that way before—and I didn't want it to stop. The uncertainties of the future didn't matter. Here and now did.

The crashing clatter from the kitchen took a few minutes to register. Nolan seemed to hear it first, spinning away from me and swearing under his breath. Without his arms I nearly collapsed, and unexpected tears sprung to my eyes. Both desolate and a little afraid, I watched him stride toward the kitchen.

He stopped, and his shoulders sagged momentarily. He drew a deep, ragged breath.

"What—what was it?" I whispered, barely audibly.

"I think," he said finally, his voice faintly husky, "that we disturbed a family of raccoons."

That wasn't all that was disturbed. My self-confidence and sense of distance both had been exploded, and I suspected Nolan felt the same.

"They're gone?"

"There's a broken pane in the window and a dozen old pots that bounced off the counters." He turned toward me with a slight smile, but I could still see the embers of fire in his eyes.

"I suppose," I said quickly, "that since there's no one here but us and some wild critters, we should get back to the house. If anyone was here, they're long gone."

He nodded thoughtfully, but I could sense the tension between us. It wasn't something I wanted to deal with right now—and apparently Nolan didn't, either.

Predictably, he told me to be careful of the loose railings along the balcony, to watch my step on the rickety stairs. And I'd certainly come to realize that I'd have to watch my step, all right, and that it wasn't just the stairs that were dangerous.

We hardly spoke on the way back to the house, both of us lost in thought—both, I'm sure, trying to ignore what had happened between us. And it couldn't be forgotten or ignored.

Stopping at the bottom of the veranda stairs, he reached out to touch my shoulder tentatively. "I should get back to the clinic." It was nearly an apology. "I'll call Jack Darling, and I'll give you a call. You'll be okay?"

"Of course."

"All right, then." He seemed reluctant to leave, but turned at last, leaving me to busy myself inside The Birches, trying to do anything but think about Nolan Chase.

I wasn't very successful.

The phone rang around seven-thirty. Nolan? I grabbed it eagerly.

There was no one there. Wrong number? Crank call? Surely nothing to worry about—but it made me feel uneasy.

When it grew dark, I built a small fire in the kitchen fireplace and sat there in Grandfather's rocker, staring at the flames, listening to the silence. Looking for a diversion, I dug out a box of old photos I'd unearthed earlier and browsed through them.

In the middle of a gaggle of flappers posed on The Birches' front porch, I saw a face that made me look more closely. She could have been my sister, she looked so much like me.

Turning the photo over, I found names. The middle girl with her beads and bangs was Adelaide Middlefield.

It was a long time before I went to bed, but though I dug through a dozen more boxes, I couldn't find out anything about Adelaide Middlefield.

Boze slept under my bed that night, a substantial dustball that snored lightly. The chronic uneasiness I'd felt ever since coming to The Birches was growing, and it kept me awake for quite a while.

Adelaide Middlefield—something my aunt had said; she'd died a violent death—and what was it about the carriage house? And I remembered the odd sensation I'd had right after Doris Taylor died, that hazy feeling of memory that had puzzled me there at The Red Finn's.

I am blessed—and cursed—with an active imagination and insatiable curiosity. The clock had struck two before I slept.

It was about eight when Boze awakened me with a couple of short barks. I opened one eye reluctantly and saw him propped with front paws on the wide windowsill, looking eagerly down over the sweep of porch roof through the gap in the middle of the curtains.

"All right," I said grudgingly. It was time to get up, anyway, though I still felt as if I hadn't even been to bed. I grabbed my robe from the footboard of the mahogany sleigh bed and walked over to open the curtains the rest of the way.

And saw Nolan's van parked below, with no sign of Nolan in or around it.

I made short work of dressing and getting ready to greet both the day and Nolan, though I hesitated in the bathroom just long enough to pull my hair back in a neat ponytail and brush a light film of blush across my cheeks. My lack of sleep showed.

What was he doing here at this hour?

By the time I'd raced downstairs and out onto the porch, Nolan was rounding the corner of the porch from the direction of the boat dock.

"Good morning," he said. "I hope I didn't wake you."

"How long have you been here?"

"Only about ten minutes. Your watchdog must have been sleeping. I thought I'd check out the dock while I waited for signs of life."

"Why didn't you knock? Ring the doorbell? Let me know you were here?"

"Well, I hated to disturb you. But this is—maybe—kind of important. I was about to get you up."

The useless watchdog was already racing circles around Nolan. "Great protection you are," I told Boze. Then, with a sudden flash of apprehension, "What brought you out here so early, anyway? What's so important? Is something wrong? Can I fix you coffee—or breakfast?"

"Nothing's really *wrong*." He didn't look directly at me. "But I stopped by for coffee early this morning at Red's, and Jack Darling came in. Something kind of strange has happened, and he mentioned that he wanted to talk to you. I told him I'd planned on picking you up for breakfast at Red's and that I'd come get you so he could tell you himself. He has all the details."

"Details of what?" The apprehension was increasing.

But the stubborn man simply shook his bull head and refused to tell me. "It's not serious, honestly. At least it doesn't sound like it. Now, lock up the house and hop in. You'll get your answers. Bring Boze along. He likes Red's front porch."

Meekly—for me—I followed his instructions. As, no doubt, he assumed that I would. There are times when curiosity beats out pride, hands down, though I was sure my cheeks had picked up color that put the blush to shame.

Nor would he answer any questions as we drove toward town.

"I told you, it's not a big thing. Just something you should know about." He shot a sideways glance at me as he pulled into the parking lot at the side of The Red Finn's. "And maybe I just wanted an excuse to come and get you, take you out for breakfast."

And maybe that sounded like a big thing in itself, but I didn't have time to think about it.

Jack was sitting at a table by the window, apparently

watching for us. Edina was busy in the kitchen, and Red took our breakfast order himself, grumbling about cooks who quit vithout notice because they vanted to go south for the vinter.

"Well, Miss Livingston—" Jack Darling began.

"Meg."

"Yes. Well, Meg, this is a funny thing. Don't know what to make of it, actually." He took a sip of coffee, and my curiosity swelled to overblown balloon size, ready to pop at any moment.

"Of *what?*" I asked tersely, and my tone made Jack smile.

"Seems old Charlie Gordon—lives out by Moose Flats— came across a wandering stranger in the forest yesterday. You'd never guess who it sounds like it was."

Maybe the same person who'd been around The Birches? I curbed my impatience and clenched my hands, waiting.

"Sounds just like it was Otis Taylor," Darling said. "His description fit Otis perfectly. Charlie said he asked him who he was and what he was doing, and the stranger just looked at him kind of vaguely and said he was trying to find out what happened to his mother."

"Good heavens!" I felt a pang of sympathy for the "stranger" wandering the woods, alone, unhappy. But I wasn't at all prepared for Jack Darling's next words.

"He also said that he was looking for a lady. That's what he said, 'a lady who let her die.' Said the lady was there, and that's why his mama was dead. Peculiar, isn't it?"

More than that. It was a little frightening. "He meant *me*? I don't understand."

"Neither did Charlie. He tried to get Otis—if that's who it was—to come see me and talk to me, but the guy just looked upset and disappeared back into the woods. Charlie thought he'd better tell me about it."

"But if he wants to see me, why doesn't he just do that? I'd be glad to talk to him."

Nolan, sitting next to me, put his hand on my shoulder. "If it's Otis, we don't really know how his mind works. Could be he's blaming you for his mother's death."

I shivered. Whether that was because of Nolan's touch or the situation, I couldn't say. "Ridiculous" I said.

"I tried calling Mr. Taylor," Jack Darling told me. "And he did confirm that Otis disappeared after his mother's funeral. Seemed pretty darned unconcerned about it, seemed to me."

Nolan muttered something about the character of Sam Taylor that I silently agreed with heartily. I stared down at the heaped plate of breakfast goodies with an appetite that had snuffed out like a candle flame in a windstorm.

"I thought you should know, so that if you should spot Otis, you could give me a quick call," Darling was saying.

But my attention had been diverted to a newcomer just arriving at the entrance to Red's.

Judd Patterson was coming up the shallow wooden steps when Boze stirred himself and sat up, ears alert and eyes sharp, to watch him approach. Boze didn't look particularly threatening, just curious, but Judd stopped abruptly and took a quick sideways step, nearly stumbling, eyeing the dog with an obvious wariness.

"Maybe he just doesn't like dogs," I said, causing both Jack Darling and Nolan to look at me strangely. "Judd," I explained, watching Judd carefully circumnavigate the area around my pussycat of a dog as if Boze were an untamed wolf.

Then he pushed through the front door, spotted us, smiled.

"Hi," he said. "Nice morning. Okay if I join you? Or is this a private conference?"

Jack Darling's friendly smile answered Judd in one way, but Nolan's slight frown—at least as seen from the corner of my eye—was not exactly welcoming.

Was Nolan just a trifle jealous? At that moment I wanted to be alone with him, to talk with him, to find out answers to many questions that would help me to know him better.

But this wasn't to be the moment. Edina hurried up behind Judd before anyone could answer.

"Oh, Nolan," she said a little breathlessly, "Mavis Amstaad called just now. Liza May finally ate something she can't handle, and she needs you."

"Mavis's goat," Nolan explained, rising and looking down at me to answer my unasked question. Goats—again? Did everyone on the north shore have goats? "Omnivorous sort. Sorry, Meg. Jack, could you run Meg back to The Birches for me?"

"I could do it," Judd offered helpfully.

"You stay and have your breakfast. Jack will do it." Nolan told him firmly.

It looked as if I weren't the only one Nolan Chase bossed around. Both Jack and Judd looked at him and nodded obediently.

I nearly threw the heavy glass sugar container at his back as he strode out the front door.

Then I sat back in the booth and laughed uncontrollably, to the surprise of the two men who looked at me as if I'd just lost my mind.

Chapter Six

"Do you keep a gun in the house, Meg?" Jack Darling asked when he pulled up in front of The Birches.

"Of course not. I couldn't shoot anything or anyone. I certainly couldn't shoot Otis Taylor, if that's what you're thinking."

"Yeah, sure. But having a gun in your hand can sometimes be a pretty darned good deterrent if someone is coming at you."

"I'll keep Boze close by."

"All right. Just be careful, hear?"

I heard. I'd heard those same words repeatedly from Nolan, from Judd, from myself. I watched Jack Darling's car bounce away over my potholed driveway and allowed myself the luxury of a deep sigh.

Suddenly I was exhausted. As a recuperative trip, this retreat to the north woods had been an utter bust.

But the exhaustion warred with restlessness. I sat in the rocking chair with Boze stretched out on the floor beside me, thinking of going back to Minneapolis, thinking of calling the office and giving George Baldwin a piece of my mind. Tactfully, of course. That problem would have to be dealt with in the near future. . . .

I must have dozed off, for my thoughts became jumbled,

and I thought I was in the carriage house and my grandmother was shushing talk about Adelaide Middlefield. I came to with a start, feeling that somehow there were answers to be found to at least some of the puzzles, if I just looked hard enough.

A few minutes later, with Boze lumbering along beside me, I climbed the rickety stairs of the carriage house. It took some prodding and poking among cobwebs, but finally, in the window seat, I found a stack of old books and journals that looked promising. My hunch had been right. I clutched them to me and headed back for the house.

Boze ran ahead of me, investigating the interesting scents at the edges of the path. I stopped suddenly, seeing the glint in the grasses, and sharply called Boze back to my side.

I was certain it hadn't been there before, though it was half hidden by sprawling vines and the long grass.

And it looked deadly.

Jack Darling had gone out toward Moose Flats, I was told when I called his office. They could get hold of him, of course.

Never mind, I said. I hung up and made sure the doors to The Birches were securely locked, then came back and dialed Nolan's number. It sounded as if the sheriff had gone out to try to find some traces of Otis Taylor, and I wished him luck. But Nolan would know about things like the vicious object that had been planted along my path, too.

He had just come in, Kate told me. When I heard his deep, reassuring voice, my knees nearly buckled in relief.

"Boze just nearly got caught in a very nasty-looking animal trap," I told him.

"*Where?*"

"Right out along the path to the carriage house. It wasn't there before. I know it wasn't. It couldn't have been."

"No, it wasn't there before. I'd have seen it, too, Meg. Keep Boze in and I'll be right there."

"Thank you," I said gratefully, but I was talking to a dead connection. He was already on his way.

I picked up the books I'd dropped helter-skelter on the floor on my dash to the phone and lined them up on the shelves under the kitchen window: a couple of books of poetry, a turn-of-the-century novel or two, an old book on Minnesota wildlife, and a simple leather-bound book with no title on the cover and gilt-edged pages.

Curious, I flipped open the dark-blue, slightly stained leather cover. In a very fine, perhaps self-consciously elegant handwriting, was the name Adelaide Middlefield. And the date: 1924. My heart did a funny little flip: here she was.

Sitting back on my heels, I riffled through the pages. A journal? Maybe there were answers here. . . .

For several minutes I sat very still, absorbed, hoping I could get to know this shadowy young woman from the past. But the sound of Nolan's van pulling around to the rear of the house finally brought me clumsily to feet that tingled from having been crumpled under me for too long. I hobbled to the door to unlock it, remembering why I had called for his help in the first place, suddenly frightened. Mysterious sounds in the night . . . the trap . . . Doris Taylor's death . . . Otis's reappearance . . . the broken window . . . all combined to threaten to blow my mental circuits.

"Meg!" He grabbed at me, understandably startled. "You look terrible. Is Boze hurt, then, after all? Where is he?"

"Boze is okay. I—I'm sorry. I just had a moment's panic, I guess." Boze's frantic barking from inside the screen door confirmed that he was at least reasonably all right. Nolan relaxed a little, though he kept his arm around me, leading me back into the kitchen.

"Easy," he said gently. "Just relax for a moment. Then you can tell me what this is all about and show me where the trap is."

I was afraid to relax. I'd probably relax right into his arms, and that might be counterproductive at this point. "The trap," I said very carefully, "is out on the path toward the carriage house." *One thing at a time*, I told myself. I led Nolan to the spot where the big trap's jaws had set its deadly teeth, waiting for a victim.

It wasn't there.

"But it was there." My voice was hollow. "I wasn't imagining things. It was right there!"

"Hmmmm. *Something* was there, all right." He cautiously moved vines aside, studying every inch of the surroundings with a single-minded intensity. "I believe you saw something. Can you describe it?"

As best I could remember, I described the heavy links, the lightly rusted metal. The mental image of those teeth closing over an animal made me shiver. And it had looked so vicious.

"I'm not making it up," I finished, hearing an edge of desperation in my voice.

"Well. . . . " There was a touch of reservation in his voice. "You couldn't describe it that well without having seen it. Unless, I suppose, you'd seen a picture of one somewhere and just *thought* you'd spotted one . . . a trick of the light?"

"But you said something had been there," I protested, angry and hurt that he was doubting me. "You saw the signs—"

"Just signs that something had been there, Meg, not a trap. And that type of trap is illegal, has been for years."

"It was there," I said stubbornly.

"All right—even assuming that it was, where did it come from, and where did it go?"

"And who would set it and then remove it? And why? Because, darn it, somebody did."

"In that case, someone's trying to frighten you, obviously. Maybe someone wants you out of The Birches." He paused for a moment, expression taut, eyes unreadable. "As I do myself, come to that. You're not safe here, Meg."

I was beginning to agree with him, but I hated to admit it. I couldn't just turn my back on the mysteries that surrounded The Birches, even if that sounded like the wisest thing to do. And I hated the doubt that I still heard behind his words.

"It couldn't be Otis." I was thinking aloud. "He just isn't that kind. He wasn't even here when the window was shot out."

"Are you sure of that?" Nolan asked. "Still, I tend to agree with you. This isn't the sort of thing Otis would do. Though we don't really know why he's come back, do we?"

We were silent for a moment. "Let's go back to the house. I'll fix coffee," I said. It sounded like such a reassuring thing to do.

"And we can talk. Maybe I can make you see reason."

"Doesn't seem to me there's much reason to see in all this."

We went up the back steps into the welcome, ordinary hominess of the big kitchen—where Boze snoozed under the table and everything seemed so wonderfully normal.

Nolan followed me over to the sink. The window over it looked down over the overgrown sweep of meadow. Clouds had come up, and a dull grayness settled over the landscape, quietly heavy and somehow ominous.

I ran water into the old graniteware coffeepot and then

set it down in the sink with exaggerated care as I felt Nolan close in behind me. His arms were on either side of me, palms down on the edge of the scarred wooden countertop, so that I couldn't move without touching him or pushing him away. And his breath stirred a living warmth at the side of my neck.

"Meg," he said, as if the words were being dragged from him, "you don't really belong here. You shouldn't be here. Leave. Go back to the city, where you belong."

"It's my house, and I do belong here," I said stubbornly, every nerve in my body aware of his nearness. "I want to find out what's going on."

"Maybe if you had somebody here with you—"

"Are you volunteering, Dr. Chase?" My voice wasn't as light as I had intended it to be.

"Don't tempt me," he groaned and turned me around to face him. His mouth descended on mine—unstoppable, insistent, greedy. I couldn't pull away; I didn't want to pull away. I wanted to return greed for greed, need for need.

The only thing that was important, at that moment, was that we were together here, in this place, at this time. Nothing else mattered, just this instant in the aeons of chaos that might swirl around us.

It was Boze who broke the spell, and afterwards I thought it was just as well that he had been there. I was on the verge of losing all control to this man who had swept me away in an emotional whirlwind, leaving all my carefully constructed defenses in splintered wreckage behind it.

But there was Boze, jealous, maybe, as devoted dogs will sometimes be. He had come from beneath the table to jump at us with both big paws, seeking attention, whining for us to include him in our peculiar game.

Nolan loosened his all-enveloping hold on me, leaning one hip against the counter, then dropping his arms to his side like dead weights. I took a deep breath through lips that felt swollen and opened reluctant eyes, trying to push away the dog with one hand. I glanced up at Nolan's face, wanting to reach out to him again.

His eyes were closed, and he breathed deeply, a little raggedly. "No," he said. The negative stabbed through me like a stilleto.

I did reach out to him. I put my hands on his arms, trying to reestablish a magic that was quickly being destroyed.

"It won't work," he said, his voice flat. "It can't work. You have to leave here, Meg. You have to go back to the city."

"You're beginning to sound like a broken record." An edge of anger was replacing that wonderful magic. "You didn't act, just now, as if you wanted me to leave."

"You don't understand."

"Suppose you explain it to me."

"Maybe I can't."

"Maybe you just aren't trying. You don't want to. You don't want anyone to see behind that oh-so-controlled mask of yours."

"Look. You're going to go back sooner or later, anyway. We both know that. And I think sooner would be better than later."

Hurt and anger combined to make me raise my voice. Boze retreated across the room, watching us warily. "Don't tell me what to do! You're right—I don't understand you at all." I stopped and drew a deep breath, and the question came out before I could stop it. "Just who was Chrissie, anyway? What did she do to you? Or maybe the question should be—what did you do to her?"

We stood frozen, all communication broken. Shutters had come back behind his eyes, and the planes of his face could have been carved from marble.

Wordlessly, he turned on his heel and walked out the door.

The rain started that night. Not a thunderous, air-clearing frenzy of rain, but a steady chill dripping, monotonous and depressing.

Even my mind seemed soggy. I couldn't decide whether I was angry with Nolan or with myself. I lay awake deep into the night, listening to the pattering of rain against the veranda roof. An occasional small gust of wind sent a few birch leaves tapping against my windows as if seeking admittance.

Nolan was right, in a way—I'd certainly had more peace of mind back in Minneapolis. And wrong, in that he was dictating to me and underestimating my sticking power. On the other hand, I had no business throwing those barbed questions about Chrissie at him. But down deep, it mattered to me what had happened between them.

We were very much attracted to each other—but did it go beyond that? I didn't know enough about him to love him, did I? And I couldn't—it just wouldn't work.

When at last I fell asleep, it was with the thought that I'd better keep my distance from Nolan Chase for a few days.

At first the rain made that easy to do. I had an unproductive and unsatisfying telephone conversation with George Baldwin, kept the coffeepot plugged in all day, overdosed on caffeine, worked on the jigsaw puzzle, and read Adelaide Middlefield's journal. Little bits and pieces of conversations overheard in childhood were trickling back: Adelaide was grandmother's sister, I thought. She'd done something "bad," apparently. What? She'd died young. Why?

She'd captured my imagination, and I could forget—for

short periods of time—about my growing attraction to Nolan Chase as I tried to track down the story of Adelaide Middlefield.

But during those wet, dreary days I secretly wished he would call. He didn't. Nothing happened: no prowlers, no noises except for the rain. No word on Otis. No Nolan.

The ambivalence I felt was cleared up for me when Boze got a burr in his ear that I couldn't seem to reach. At first he'd seemed to enjoy the rain, dashing out through the underbrush and chasing wet shadows, then coming in to shake himself all over the kitchen.

Then he started worrying at his left ear, and though I parted the matted damp fur and tried to help him, I couldn't locate the source of the trouble—and Boze made it clear that he didn't even want me to try. When the ear started to fester and poor old Boze began shaking his head, whining, I bit the bullet and called for an appointment with the only local veterinarian.

"Good thing you brought him in. This could turn into a general infection—he does seem a little feverish." Nolan's strong hands were expertly and tenderly exploring the left side of Boze's head, and worshipful Boze wasn't even whimpering.

Well, that was why I'd brought him, of course, to be taken care of. But my dog was on better terms with Nolan than I was, and I was uncomfortably certain that was partly—or more than partly—my fault.

I don't handle guilt well. I swallowed hard and looked at everything in the office except Nolan. "I was afraid it might be serious. Can you treat it?"

"No problem. It's close to the surface and—there. Good boy." Boze gave only a token yip and then grinned doggily at Nolan before whimpering slightly and laying his head with infinite weariness back down on the examining table. "Hmmmmm. Well, Boze, old boy, how would you like to spend the night here?"

"You mean I have to leave him?"

"I think it might be wise. I'll give him a shot of anti-biotics, and that should do it—but I'd really like to keep an eye on him. I could bring him back to you tomorrow morning, if he seems to be recovering."

"That's too much to ask. I'll pick him up."

"We can talk about that when the time comes." His tone was cool, polite, professional, and he didn't seem to want to look directly at me any more than I could handle looking directly at him.

But he was stroking Boze with a caring hand, looking at the dog with concern and compassion. He was, after all, a sensitive and gentle man. I felt a growing warmth wrap itself around my heart.

"I think," I said carefully, "that I probably owe you an apology."

"Really?" He turned away to wash his hands, so that I couldn't see his face. "Maybe not. I know I tend to be overbearing at times. At least, that's what I've been told by people who think they know me well."

"It's not that, and you know it. I shouldn't have snapped at you about Chrissie. That's none of my business. It's just that I didn't know how to handle the way you—the way I—the situation between us—and I just lashed out." *Lame, Meg,* I told myself, *but maybe he understands*.

There was an uncomfortable silence. I could hear the monotonous dripping of the rain from the eaves outside. He didn't understand. He didn't want to understand. I didn't understand, either. Maybe there *wasn't* any "situation" between us, after all.

But I couldn't be that mistaken. . . .

He turned back to me, his expression carefully neutral. "I think we do need to talk, Meg. But somewhere away from The Birches. In—neutral surroundings."

"Yes," I said, inadequately.

"Maybe we can go up to Grand Marais for dinner one night soon. There's a great restaurant up there." He hesitated, as if uncharacteristically unsure of himself. "Anyway, if you'd like to, before you go back to the city?"

"Yes." He was still assuming I'd be going back soon. And I wasn't going back until I had some answers. A lot of answers, to a lot of questions.

"I'll bring Boze back tomorrow morning, if he's better," Nolan said. "And if you're free on Friday evening for dinner—well, we'll talk about it."

"Thank you. My social schedule up here doesn't seem to be overextended, so that would be very nice." I could be as cool and polite as he was, though it was an effort. "Thank you. I'll get on back to The Birches then and leave Boze in your tender, loving care." I reached out to give my canine companion a loving rub. "You be a good boy," I told him and turned to leave.

Nolan's voice stopped me at the door. "Be sure and lock up securely tonight. I don't like to think of you out there in that house without even Boze with you."

"Quit worrying," I answered, looking back over my shoulder at him with a touch of my old exasperation at being told what to do. "There's really nothing to hurt me back at The Birches. Nothing at all."

"Well, call me if you have any problems."

"Sure." Since he seemed to be one of my major problems, that was rather useless advice. Still, I appreciated it.

It rained more heavily that night, and though the steady downpour had let up by morning, the world was gray and sodden, and the heavy atmosphere hung dismally over the forests.

Every branch, every blade of grass—even every thought that went through my mind—seemed to be weighted downward.

I missed Boze. I'd slept raggedly, even after a snifter of brandy and listening, eyes closed, to an old recording of Granddad's of Dvorak's *New World Symphony*. It had been lulling. It had been peaceful. But I wasn't at all sleepy.

The house creaked. All night. The humidity, of course, seeping into the old joists and rafters. . . .

Feeling heavy-lidded, I had three cups of scalding coffee and a huge bowl of vitamin-enriched, energy-boosting cereal. At least that's what it said on the box. I couldn't see much improvement in my energy.

Was it worry about Boze or just a gnawing desire to hear Nolan's voice that made me want to call the clinic? I decided it was both and grabbed for the phone.

It was Nolan's voice that answered; maybe Kate wasn't there yet. I was glad it was Nolan. "How's Boze?" I asked abruptly, not even identifying myself.

"Meg Livingston, I presume," said the amused voice at the other end. "Boze is fine. How is Meg?"

"Meg misses Boze." It all sounded so silly that I chuckled in spite of myself. "I'm glad he's fine. Can he come home?"

"I would think so. I just gave him another shot, and he's eating with what seems to be an excellent appetite, and his tail seems to have recovered its wag."

"That's my dog. I'm so glad. I'll come get him right away."

"Don't bother. I'll bring him out as soon as he finishes eating. I'll have to go down to the store to buy more dog food, anyway, from the way it looks."

"I don't want to put you out, and I'll buy more dog food."

"Meg, you're being silly. Please don't worry about it. You must be missing him quite a bit."

"Actually, I am." I wasn't used to being called silly, but I supposed he was right, in a way.

"I'll be by in just a short time, then."

I hung up feeling slightly better. Boze would be here soon. Nolan would be here soon. And maybe, in the break in the rain, a brisk walk down toward the boat dock would do me good.

Even boots and jeans and a windbreaker didn't keep the dampness out of my bones, though. Lake Birchleaf lay dully silver and quiet under the heavy air—no ripples, no birds, no frogs sounding off in the reeds. Still as death, the thought came unbidden into my mind.

I thought something moved in the underbrush, and I suddenly felt very alone and exposed. I turned and retreated to the relative safety of the house, heart pounding.

And stopped abruptly just inside the back door, holding my breath. Toward the front of the house, there were sounds. Someone was there, walking around quietly, opening and closing doors, looking for something—for me?

Nolan—with Boze? But Nolan would have come around the outside of the house looking for me, probably, would have called my name, and Boze would have barked, and—

The sound came again. Tentative, secretive noises. Who? Not Nolan. Otis? But why?

The noises ceased. I reached over to the shelf beside the stove and grabbed the heavy old wood-and-metal meat tenderizer, weighing it carefully in a hand that shook slightly. A good weapon—if I got a chance to swing, if I needed to swing.

I tiptoed across the kitchen floor nearly soundlessly. Still no furtive scuttlings from the front of the house. Could I have imagined that I'd heard something?

No. Something moved, a scraping, a footstep.

I slipped through the butler's pantry with the tenderizer raised like a tomahawk, through the gloomy shadows of the shuttered dining room, sidling at last through the arch that led into the hallway. Holding my breath.

And stopping dead in my tracks when the dark, shapeless mass beyond the door moved and took human form.

Chapter Seven

He stood there, a wizened elderly man in a damp tweed cap, frightened eyes peering out from behind wire-framed spectacles, and one of the heavy family candlesticks raised in a hand that shook visibly.

"Who—who the devil are you?" he asked, in a voice that shook worse than his hand.

"Stand still," I commanded, though he showed no signs of doing anything else, if his shaking was discounted. "This is my house. Who are you?"

"Your—house?" The hand holding the candlestick fell to his side, and he peered at me suspiciously. "Yours?"

"Mine. I'm Margaret Livingston."

"Oh, horse puckey."

His shoulders sagged inside his old weatherproof jacket, and his expression was so lugubrious that I nearly laughed, but managed to continue looking stern and invincible, I hoped.

"I'm Will Stiverson," he added. "From Two Harbors?" He looked at me hopefully, still keeping his distance.

I leaned against the wall with sheer relief.

"The man who checks on the house."

"Yup. Regular as clockwork, I am. You should have let me know you'd be here. Coulda scared me right into a heart attack."

"Sorry. But you scared me, too, you know." I recognized his name; I'd sent him checks since Mother died.

"Well, I knew somebody was here. Things had been moved around. But I didn't see your car." He still sounded slightly suspicious. I couldn't blame him.

"It's out in back." We fell silent for a moment, both regaining equilibrium, I suppose, and I could hear a car coming toward The Birches. Through the heavy leaded windows that framed the front door across the great hall, I could see Nolan's van. Thank goodness.

Will Stiverson had taken his cap off and was murmuring something reproachful about driving all the way up here for nothing. I ignored him, walking across the hallway to watch Nolan and Boze come up the steps and across the veranda.

Nolan glanced back over his shoulder curiously at Stiverson's battered compact, which had been pulled in close to the curve of the veranda.

"You have company?" Nolan asked when I opened the door, then saw Will Stiverson standing in the arch of the doorway. Boze brushed past Nolan, short yips questioning the presence of a stranger.

But he was glad enough to see me again that he was willing to ignore the presence of what he apparently considered to be a pretty innocuous intruder when I called him to me. He huddled next to my leg to watch the proceedings.

"Mr. Stiverson is the man who comes to check on the house," I told Nolan. "We—sort of scared each other."

"Wasn't scared at all," Will Stiverson scoffed, transferring his cap to his left hand and holding his right out to Nolan. "Hi there. Nice dog you've got there."

"Meg's dog. I'm her vet. Or, rather, I'm the dog's vet—Nolan Chase. Glad to meet you."

"Look, I'll make some coffee," I offered. "After you've come all this way, Mr. Stiverson, you probably need a cup."

"Wouldn't go amiss," he nodded, apparently forgiving me for having scared the horse puckey out of him.

"Can you stay, too, Nolan?"

He glanced at his watch. "For a short time, thanks." He looked back up at Stiverson, a thoughtful frown pulling his eyebrows together, and we trooped more or less silently back to the kitchen, Boze happily bringing up the rear and heading for his favorite spot under the table.

I wondered what had brought that look to Nolan's face.

I found out almost immediately. "You've never found anything suspicious here at The Birches when you've been here before? Things out of place, signs of transients, anything like that?" he asked.

I was pouring coffee into Nolan's cup and hesitated, looking back and forth at the two men's faces. It was a good question, and I waited for the answer.

"Course not. If I had, I woulda reported it, wouldn't I? It's a creepy old place, though. Nothing here but a few old ghosts, probably." He laughed, humorlessly, with a touch of uncertainty. "I'd let someone know right away if I thought anyone had broken in. Why? You think you got intruders?"

Well, of course he would have let me know of any problems. I turned away to put the pot back on the range. When I turned back, a peculiar glint had come into Will Stiverson's eyes.

He was staring at the kitchen fireplace, shaking his head slightly, looking as if he'd just remembered something. An uneasy feeling made the back of my neck prickle as if an invisible ghoulie were tickling it with a feather.

"Not to say some small animal couldn't have made its way in sometime, I suppose. I mean, I think maybe they did."

"Why?" I asked, a little breathless.

"Why not? To get out of the rain or something, I suppose."

"No—I mean why do you think an animal came in at all?"

"Wellll," he drawled. "Funny thing, it was."

"What was?" Nolan asked with an edge of impatience.

"Been a long time ago, and nothing's happened since then."

"*What* was a long time ago? How long ago? What are you talking about?"

Nolan heard the thin thread of tension in my voice and reached across the table to put a large, warm hand over mine. Not many weeks before, I'd have retrieved my hand and given Nolan an icy smile to tell him I could handle things, thanks. Right now I just settled for a half smile that wasn't at all icy.

And of course I left my hand right where it was. It felt good there.

"Start at the beginning," Nolan suggested, "and tell us what exactly happened."

"Sure, that's what I was about to do, wasn't it? One time—I think about three years ago, not long after I started looking after the place—I found one of the windows jammed open. There. Over the range." Automatically, all three of us looked at the window over the range, which was, of course, perfectly normal. "Looked to me like a small animal of some kind might have crawled through. A little messy, it was."

"What do you mean, 'a little messy'? The window? The kitchen?" I asked tightly. Nolan's hand tightened over mine. I swallowed hard and tried to chase away the stubborn ghoulie with the feather. After all, whatever it was that Will Stiverson had seen, it was—as he had said—a long time ago and couldn't have anything to do with my recent problems.

"Nothing missing, Miss Livingston," he said. "Or damaged or anything like that. But there were towels dragged onto the floor and a funny stain over by the fireplace."

"The kitchen fireplace?" Nolan asked.

Will Stiverson nodded. "Right over there, on the hearth, but I cleaned it up good. It—well, it looked as if it coulda been bloodstains, and I figured an injured raccoon or something had got in. Of course, it did make me a little leery, but I checked every room in the house, like I always do, and nobody was here—live or dead, far's I could tell. Besides, ghosts don't bleed, from what I've heard, so I figured it wasn't a ghost."

"Logical," Nolan said calmly. "I'm sure you were right—it was probably, as you thought, just a small animal."

"And it never happened since," Will Stiverson said, and I heard a hint of relief in his voice that he wasn't going to be raked over the coals for not reporting the incident. He stopped and a growing puzzlement spread over his features, bringing curiosity to the gray eyes that studied us through the strong lenses of his glasses. "Now, why did you ask me about that in the first place? You had trouble out here recently, maybe?"

"Not really," Nolan said cheerfully before I could answer. "Just wanted to make sure you hadn't seen signs of anyone hanging around. You know how it is these days—can't trust anybody, can you? Never know what kind of lowlife might be crawling around in the bushes."

Stiverson laughed—a near cackle—and nodded vehemently. "You got it, Doc. Well, I might as well take off. Starting to rain again, and as long as everything is all right here—How long are you going to be here, young woman?"

"I'm—not sure. I'll get in touch with you when I decide. Thank you for being such a good watchman, Mr. Stiverson."

He left, giving us a last grin over his shoulder, all his frightened and ruffled feathers back once again in place.

As were mine. Except—

"Why didn't you want to tell him we thought we had prowlers?" I asked as we turned to go back into the house.

"We?" Nolan asked innocently. "*You're* the one with the prowlers. And we don't know that there are any, really."

"Well, *something's* going on."

"Ummmm. It looks that way. What bothers me is that I don't know whether someone is after you—or something in the house."

"But, in either case, why me? Why now?"

"We don't know. But since you're too stubborn to leave, we may find out the hard way. I don't like it."

There was a gentle caring in his voice that set off singing vibrations deep inside me. He really cared what happened to me.

Our eyes met, and an invisible aura of magic wrapped around us. Caught in its spell, I took a step toward him just as the phone began to shrill insistently.

It cut through the magic like a machete. "All right," I said to the phone. "All right."

I resisted the overpowering urge to rip the darned thing off the wall and managed to answer in a fairly normal voice. "For you," I told Nolan. "Sounds like Kate." And of course it had to be some kind of emergency, and of course he had to leave. . . .

"Friday evening," he said, hanging up and turning back to me. He reached out and let a finger trace a fiery path down my cheek, my jawline, my throat, a halfsmile softening the angles of his face. "Friday evening will be ours. I'll call you."

He let himself out the back door and was gone, and I stood for a long time staring out at the dripping woodlands, lost in thought. Thoughts about Adelaide Middlefield, about Otis Taylor, about animals in my kitchen . . . about Nolan. About myself.

Nothing about this trip was turning out the way I'd planned it. Not at all.

I was beginning to like the forests.

No longer did it seem that there was danger hidden behind every tree trunk. If there was danger, it wasn't, I realized, the fault of the forest. Instead, I had the eerie feeling that the trees, the entire woodland, was reaching out arms to protect me.

It was a very odd feeling.

The afternoon after Will Stiverson's unexpected visit, Boze and I made another trip to the carriage house.

During the morning I'd browsed through Adelaide's journals. They weren't complete. She'd been somewhat bored at the beginning of the summer, then apparently met someone who made it a much more interesting summer than she had expected.

As I had, for that matter. We had more in common than our appearance.

I knew there were more books in the compartment in the window seat in the carriage house, and I hoped there would be another of Adelaide Middlefield's journals. I'd learned about all I could from the one I'd brought into the house with me.

And I did find another journal, along with a couple of scrapbooks. I slipped them under my windbreaker to protect them from the gusty showers and hurried back to the house.

In one of the downstairs cubbyholes, I'd found a boxful of papers, and it seemed to me there was another scrapbook in there. And more old photos. It seemed important, suddenly, to put them all together and go through them. I piled everything onto the kitchen table and started in.

Two hours later I had a few tentative answers, and I had many new, disturbing questions.

Adelaide Middlefield, young, spirited, full of life, had indeed found someone to alleviate her "boredom" in the summer of 1924. And before the summer was over, she was dead—and so was her father. And I still didn't have the full story.

The yellowed obituaries from the Duluth papers I'd found told me little: they died on the same day. One news clipping hinted at suicide and murder, another just said "accident." I found another picture of Adelaide and one of her father, who'd been—let's see—my great grandfather? Sounded right. Murder? Suicide? But why? Maybe there had been a local newspaper then—maybe I could find out more. I'd have to ask Nolan. I was sure there was more to the story, and I had to know.

"Hey," Nolan said appreciatively when I met him at the door on Friday evening. "No jeans. You look terrific."

No wonder he looked a little surprised. I'd been wearing grubbing-around-in-the-attic clothes ever since I'd arrived, and I hadn't brought much else. I hadn't anticipated anything as interesting as social life up here—as interesting as Nolan Chase. The silver-gray silk shirt, my gray cashmere cardigan, a soft heathery tweed skirt, and my black Italian pumps were the closest thing to "formal" that I'd lugged along. And I'd spent as much time on makeup and hair as I normally spent for important hostessing chores at the North

Star. Tonight I didn't want Nolan commenting that my eyes looked like holes in a shroud, thanks.

I gave him a once-over in return. "Hey," I told him, "no lab coat and work shirt. You look pretty terrific yourself." He did, too, in shirt and tie and a subdued sport jacket that seemed to accentuate the breadth of his shoulders.

He smiled back and watched as I stepped over to the library table to pick up my small black bag. When I turned back to him, he had walked silently up behind me and was studying the array of old photos on the table. I'd made up a "rogue's gallery" of old family photos—Adelaide, of course, included.

"Family? Wow." He picked up the snapshot of Adelaide. "Family, all right. You look a lot like her. Who was she?"

"A great-aunt, as nearly as I can figure. There's some kind of mystery there. I want to talk to you about her. Later."

"*Another* mystery? Okay." He grinned at me. "Where's Boze?"

"In the kitchen." Muffled short yipes from the back of the house confirmed it, and Nolan smiled and stepped closer.

With one finger, he brushed a stray hair back off my forehead, and I could feel the attraction between us gathering force once again with a magnetic warmth.

He bent and kissed me lightly on the lips. "Ready?" he asked, his breath mingling with mine.

"Oh, yes," I agreed, with more feeling than I had intended.

For a moment he hesitated, then drew back reluctantly and opened the front door for me. There was both withdrawal and promise in the gesture.

We were both rather silent on the drive up to Grand Marais. A few comments on the seemingly unending drizzle, which splattered against the windshield just enough to obscure vision and make the windshield wipers necessary; a few comments on how leaden and gray Lake Superior seemed under the heavy evening sky.

Both of us were uneasily aware, I think, that this would be an important, possibly difficult, evening. Not just a casual dinner date, but a time for facing problems and clearing the air.

"Quiet today out there," Nolan said, breaking a short silence as the road wound along a clear spot above the inland sea. "But in storms the waves reach the tops of the bluffs. Dangerous."

I felt an involuntary shiver. I hadn't walked the beaches or the bluffs since Doris Taylor had died. "Yet it can be so beautiful. So deceptive. . . ."

"When you're ready to walk along the bluffs or the beaches again, I'll go with you. It might make it easier." His voice was very gentle, and I was surprised that he'd understood my feelings so accurately. "We'll pick the right time, and it'll work out all right. You'll get over the fear."

A warm gratitude for his understanding flowed through me. The prickles of resentment I might have felt just a few weeks before were gone completely: I didn't want to snap that I could handle any fears I might have quite nicely on my own. I *wanted* Nolan with me. *Watch it, Meg Livingston, you're mellowing out,* I warned myself sternly. But mellowing was so nice.

"That's it," he said a moment later, flipping on the turn signals and indicating a cluster of lights twinkling in the dusky dampness. "Small place, but the best food on the north shore."

The parking lot was crowded, but inside there was warmth and an immediate welcome. They seemed to know Nolan well, and within minutes we were seated close to the small dance floor with the waiter saying yes, Dr. Chase, we do have the trout this evening.

And I hadn't missed the look of curious interest the hostess had shot my way when she led us back into the crowded dining room.

"The trout," Nolan told me, dismissing the waiter with a smile and a request for a wine I recognized as being one of the more expensive on our North Star wine list, "is what we'll have. It's steamed with wine and butter and served with herbed wild rice, fresh local mushrooms, and an orange-cranberry relish that's fantastic."

He stopped suddenly, caught, perhaps, by the expression on my face. I was close to laughter, and I think I was shaking my head just a little. The Boss had taken over again, hadn't he? "Unless you don't think you'd like it?" he said, and I knew he felt that particular thought was literally unthinkable.

"It sounds wonderful," I said demurely, and it did. Let him order. This was his show.

Our conversation during dinner was carefully impersonal, though the wine helped ease the tension between us. He asked questions about my work, and I told him: about having to know every phase of the running of a large hotel, from maintenance and clerical staffs to housekeeping and banquet planning.

"Sounds as if you're indispensable."

I laughed a little wryly. "Wish I were. I'd assumed I'd be taking over management next year, but the current manager seems to be taking advantage of my absence to work up his good-old-boy network. He's pulled an old crony from middle management to fill my place while I'm gone. I don't like the look and feel of it."

Nolan's eyebrows lifted. "Sounds as if you'll have to go back and fight for your rights."

"I may. I love my work. . . . " My voice trailed off, and I took a sip of the excellent wine. I loved The Birches, too, and I still had all those questions that needed to be answered. And—admit it!—I wondered if I was beginning to love Nolan, too.

It wasn't until we reached dessert—apple tarts with heavy cream, and heavenly aromatic coffee—that Nolan began to look a little subdued, thoughtful. A seriousness settled over his wonderful granite-carved features.

"I have to tell you about Chrissie," he said bluntly.

"Not if you don't want to," I said hastily. *But I'll kill you if you don't,* added a determined voice in my mind. "I should never have brought it up—thrown it at you the way I did."

"No, you shouldn't." Thank goodness I could detect a hint of a smile behind the words. "But since you did, I think you should know. Chrissie and I were married fresh out of school. It lasted all of six months, and then she left. Just like that. We were divorced several months later. That was six years ago."

The bare bones of a story and the shadow of an old pain in his eyes. "I'm so sorry," I said. "It must have been difficult."

He was switching the salt and pepper shakers back and forth, and I think he hardly heard me. "She was from Chicago," he went on quietly, staring down at the shakers— back and forth, back and forth. "City born and bred. Young, full of life and not meant for the long, silent nights of the north. It was—impossible."

"Look," I tried, feeling a little desperate. "You don't have to tell me all this." Yet I was beginning to understand, and I wanted to reach out to him and try to soothe the hurt away.

"I loved her," he said simply, looking up from the salt

and pepper shakers and into my eyes with a penetrating intensity. "I loved her deeply. She really didn't give it much of a chance. . . . "

"And you couldn't pull up stakes and set up a practice near a city." He looked as if he were about to defend himself, as if I were criticizing, but I wasn't. "No," I said, "I know that you couldn't. Not just that you wouldn't, but that you couldn't."

He sat back in his chair, coffee cup in hand, staring at me over the edge of it. "So now you know what my problem is," he said. "And you, Meg Livingston, certainly haven't made life any easier for me." His voice dropped, and he looked away from me. "Because the moment I saw you, I started to fall in love—with another city woman. One who has even more reason than Chrissie ever had to go back to the city. At least Chrissie wasn't in any danger up here, and I believe that you are."

I put my own coffee cup carefully back in its saucer, numbed into speechlessness—certainly not a normal condition for me—by his words.

"Oh, Nolan," I said after what seemed to be an eternal pause. At that moment everything seemed so hopeless, so confusing. I wanted to tell him that I shared his feelings, but couldn't quite make myself say it. "What on earth do we do now?"

He sighed. "Wouldn't it be a good idea, Meg, for you to close up The Birches for the winter? To go back to Minneapolis, clear up your problems at the hotel, and come back in the spring to do whatever you have to do to get the house ready for the market? It'll sell better then, too."

It was as if he'd never mentioned love at all. He'd admitted to it, and now, partly because of my response—or lack of it—he was deliberately putting the admission behind him.

"No," I said, "that wouldn't be a good idea. I want to stay." I looked at him levelly. "There are a lot of things here that have to be worked out. And that includes our feelings for each other, doesn't it?"

He looked startled. I'd brought him back to the starting point, and he hadn't expected it. Then a slow, warming smile lit his face, his eyes, and he reached one hand across the table to grasp mine. "Oh, Marvelous Meg," he said, "I want very much to talk about our feelings. But right now I want to dance with you. And later—later, we'll talk. . . . "

But could we talk our way around the difficulties? The music was slow, and the floor was crowded, and I had the sneakiest of suspicions that our dancing together was not going to rid us of our "problems," either.

It didn't.

We danced well together, the rhythms of our pulses and the music melding us in a wonderful warmth, and I didn't want the music to end. But, of course, it must. For now.

Chapter Eight

We left after only a couple of dances.

Both of us, I think, felt the awkward constraints that we'd put on ourselves—the holding back, the admission of futility, the wall of hard facts we had to face.

I could not be falling in love with Nolan Chase, whatever my body and soul were telling me. There wasn't any future in it. And I very much doubted if we could be just friends.

A gusty wind had come up while we were in the restaurant, and heavy sluices of rain cut through the glare of the headlights. Nolan drove slowly and with tremendous assurance—the way he did everything, but he had to be used to bleak changes of weather along these shores, didn't he?

Unconsciously, I sighed deeply. Bleak was such a good description of the way I felt.

"Tired, Meg?"

"No. Yes. A little. It's partly the weather. Will it stay like this all through the autumn? Rain and wind? Pretty dismal."

"We'll have some beautiful Indian-summer days yet—but this must be depressing for you, shut up in that big place of yours."

"Actually, it's great weather for repacking boxes and sorting things. I'll give some things to charity, and I'm going to call an antique dealer I know in Duluth about some

111

of the furniture—and I'm going to strip out carpets so the floors can be redone and the walls painted, and—'' I was babbling. I caught myself and added, almost defensively, ''Don't worry. I can stay busy.''

''Mmmmmm. I don't doubt that.'' Was he laughing at me? ''Let me know if there's anything I can do to help, won't you?''

''Of course. Thank you.''

''Good. You're welcome.''

A mile's worth of silence, and we'd reached the rutted road that led off to Lake Birchleaf. The wind howled through the overgrown branches, and Nolan slowed to a crawl, easing his van as gently as possible over the water-filled potholes.

''I'd hate to have to be outside in all this,'' I said. ''Glad I left Boze in the kitchen and not out on the porch.''

I stopped abruptly as I saw the patch of white at the side of the road. A face stared from under a dripping cap, eyes wide, frightened. Then it turned frantically away, arms thrashing at undergrowth, and disappeared into the darkness of the forest.

''Who was that?'' Nolan said. ''Did you see him?'' He came to an abrupt halt, staring intently toward the point where the apparition had vanished.

''Yes, I saw him,'' I answered, a deep feeling of pity welling up in my heart. Pity—mixed with just a touch of fear. ''It was Otis Taylor.'' I eased open the car door, letting in a gust of wind and a smattering of raindrops, calling Otis's name into the darkness. There was no answer.

Nolan grabbed a flashlight from under the seat and headed around the van on a run. ''Stay put,'' he flung over his shoulder. ''Stay in the van.''

Reluctantly, I obeyed. It *was* Otis, wasn't it? On some deep level, I didn't believe that Otis Taylor was a threat to me. But until I could talk to him, I wouldn't know that for a certainty. If only he weren't so shy of contact. . . .

I didn't have much time to worry about it. Nolan was back in just a moment's time, shaking water off like a big dog. "He could have headed any direction," he said, getting back in the van. "No sense in even trying to find him in the dark—in this weather."

"Poor Otis. Oh, the poor, wet, cold soul."

"He's not a child, Meg," Nolan said sharply. "And we don't know what he's up to. Let's get up to the house."

"But he is a child, Nolan, mentally and emotionally. And I can't believe he'd want to harm me," I shot back.

"Look, Meg. Things have been going on here that we don't understand. The trap, the footprints, the window—they could have been Otis's doing."

"They weren't. I'm sure of it." But I wasn't sure, was I? There had been that little frisson of fear when I'd seen him, white-faced as a ghost beside the road.

Thank goodness I had left the light on outside the front door. It was a small, warm pool of reassurance.

"I'm going in with you," Nolan said.

I didn't argue. It sounded like a good idea, all things considered.

Getting Boze from the kitchen, we checked all the ground-floor rooms. From the way Boze was acting—wildly happy at seeing both of us—it didn't appear anyone had been anywhere near the house. But there was a new leak around one of the windows in the dining room. "Another job for Joe," Nolan said. "I'll let him know."

"Thanks—and I'll make coffee," I suggested. Then, tentatively, "If you'd like to have some?"

"I'd like. He could still come to the house, you know. It might be a good idea if I stayed for just a little while."

Was I wrong, or was there a tone in his voice that hinted

he was glad he had an excuse for staying—for just a little while? He followed me into the kitchen and watched as I set up the pot.

"I wish he *would* come to the house. He's a lost soul." I thought for a moment, then took a tray from the cupboard. "If we have coffee in the parlor bay, we can see two directions—with the veranda light on, we might see him if he came back this way."

He nodded agreement and took the loaded tray from me when the coffee was ready, and we trailed back through the gloomy rooms to the parlor.

There was a large, round marble-topped table in the bay and two heavily carved dark chairs on either side. I turned on the low-voltage candle lights on either side of the bay, then stood for a moment staring out at the impenetrable night.

Behind me, reflected in the distorting glass, I could see Nolan unloading the tray, watching me at the same time. And in the forest—a slight movement? Probably just the wind.

He continued to watch me thoughtfully—unnervingly silent—even after we had settled on either side of the table. I was glad it was a good-sized table; it put some needed distance between us.

"Look," he said at last, "I know a developer—Martin Simms. I could get in touch with him—"

"Please don't. Not right now. When I'm really ready, I'll talk to him—or to Judd Patterson. I just don't want to let go of this place quite yet. It's—it's part of the family."

He shrugged, laughing a little. "Crazy family. But I do understand."

"And there are things I would like to find out about this crazy family. Maybe you can help."

"I'll try."

"In 1924, there were two deaths here. That young woman you said looked like me—she died suddenly, and so did her father. On the same day. My grandmother refused to talk about it, and I can't find much information on what actually happened. Was there a county newspaper back then? Would there be any way of checking it? Have you ever heard any old stories about it?"

"No," he said thoughtfully. "It doesn't sound familiar, but that was a long time ago. And yes, I think probably you could find something in the county archives. There are a lot of great old stories and legends about this area, actually. I'm going down to Langston tomorrow afternoon, do you want me to check for you? You could always do it yourself, of course, but I know the town staff and the editor of the paper. And there are a few old-timers left who might remember something."

That may have been the first time that Nolan Chase admitted that I could do things for myself, if I wanted to. He was learning. Yet he *could*, as he hinted, probably get to the facts sooner than I could. "Would you do that?" I was beginning to feel a stirring of excitement, and it showed in my voice. "It's just curiosity, you understand—just part of the house's history that I'd like to know more about."

"Hmmmm. Yes. Something about the story makes me curious, too. A local scandal. I'll look it up."

And while he was checking old newspaper records, I'd read more of Adelaide's journals and dig in the attic trunks, and maybe—just maybe—I could find some answers.

I lay awake a long time that night.

Nolan had left me with just a peck on the cheek. I felt let down, but what could I expect? He was holding himself back, just as I was.

I stared at the ceiling, lecturing myself. *A fine mess you've gotten yourself into, Meg Livingston! You really care about him, and he seems to care about you, and it just won't work! Your future is with the North Star. His is here in Caribou Bay.*

Was there any way to work this out?

At one A.M., at three A.M., there were no answers to that question.

Boze seemed restless, and I heard the house breathing and settling and creaking around me. The rain had stopped, but it was cold . . . poor Otis. I wanted to help him, and didn't know how.

I fell asleep to be haunted by dreams of Otis, and Adelaide, and we were all being stalked through The Birches by an animal that looked suspiciously like Red's Kitty.

The sun was actually making tentative attempts to break through the clouds the next morning. After breakfast I took Boze for a short walk along the waterlogged paths around The Birches, watching rainbows dance in the drops of water on every leaf and branch. Surely all this was a good sign? If the weather cleared, would some of the questions clear up, too?

The phone was ringing insistently when Boze and I let ourselves in the back door. I shut him and his muddy paws in the small enclosed porch and hurried to answer, hoping it might be Nolan, that it wasn't another of those calls with no one there, that it wasn't bad news of some kind—but why should it be?

"Ah," said Nolan's voice, sounding relieved, on the other end in answer to my slightly breathless hello. "I was about to give up. Glad I got through."

"Boze and I took a little walk. I just got in."

"Probably a good thing you went this morning. It's going to rain again this afternoon."

Killjoy. "Did you call to give me the weather report? How thoughtful."

"Nope. Not really. I called to tell you that Red saw Otis early this morning, rummaging through the refuse cans behind the inn. Red yelled at him, but Otis took off. He managed to follow Otis a little way into the woods and thinks he knows where he's holed up. Jack Darling's going to check it out."

"I hope they find him—that somebody finds him. He must be so cold and hungry and wet."

"Your sympathy's kind and generous, but keep your distance. We still don't know what he's after. Might be best if you stayed very close to The Birches until Jack has had a chance to try to bring Otis back to civilization."

"I suppose you're right." A short time ago I would probably have made a comment about Caribou Bay not exactly being in the center of civilization, but now I managed, with just a touch of difficulty, to bite my tongue. "I'll watch for him and call the sheriff's office if I see him."

"Good. I'll be in touch later today."

I realized when I hung up that the sun had indeed disappeared behind another bank of clouds. Well, I'd just have to make the most of it. I got Boze's muddy paws cleaned off, had some lunch, and piled all the family papers on the kitchen table once again.

An hour later I hadn't made much headway. Adelaide's early-summer boredom had been relieved when she went to a tea at a big house down the coast and met someone smooth, smart, and handsome named Max. She liked Max. Max was spiffy. Max was the bee's knees. *For some reason,* she had written at the end of the last journal, *Daddy is being a complete fuddy-duddy. He doesn't like Max. So silly. I won't let it bother me.*

That was just a few days before the two deaths. Had she written more in a new journal? She'd apparently stashed her writings in the carriage house. Maybe I'd better go check again, just in case. Maybe I'd missed something.

A heavy mist hung in the air, and I left Boze in the house. I'd only be gone for a few moments, after all. I threw my raincoat over my shoulders and, for an uncertain moment, wished Nolan were with me.

The weathered outside staircase at the carriage house was slick with rain, and I went up carefully. The unlocked door gave easily under my hand. Was—was there a noise, some-where in the murky light, over toward the kitchen? Of course not. Just the wind. But there must be a leak in the roof, because there was a filmy puddle of dampness in front of the door to the kitchen.

I slipped over to the window seat and lifted the lid. Yes, there was a slim book in there and some loose papers. I slipped the papers into the book and turned back toward the door. And saw the footprint just beyond that wet spot—a footprint in the kitchen that was never made by a raccoon. "Otis?" I tried tentatively, but there was no answer.

Fear took over. For some reason I was very sure it wasn't Otis in the carriage house. Grasping the book, I tiptoed out of the door and headed for the stairs. With a little luck I'd get back to the house and call Jack Darling.

No such luck. Instead, there was a feeling of weight coming down hard on my right shoulder, a stumbling, a groping for a wooden rail that shuddered, cracked, and gave way under my left hand. And then the terrible sensation of falling. It seemed forever, it seemed like a split second—and then darkness.

There was a gentle hand cradling the back of my head, another brushing hair from my forehead. I struggled against the unnatural weight of gravity that lay across my eyelids, with little success.

"Don't try to move." Nolan's voice, quiet and reassuring and at the same time deeply concerned. "Just relax."

"Thank goodness," I managed, but for the moment couldn't say anything else. *Thank goodness you're here, thank goodness I'm alive.* Opening my eyes took tremendously concentrated effort, but I managed. I wanted to see Nolan.

He swam into focus, kneeling there on the damp ground beside me, with a tender, intense look in his eyes that, under other circumstances, I might have suspected was love. And beside him was Boze, sitting close with his head on one side, looking at me with worried devotion.

I felt a slight smile lift the corners of my mouth. Darned dog had the same look in his eyes as Nolan. So much for love.

And, blurrily, behind the two of them, slouch hat pushed back on his head and leaning forward to examine me assessingly, I saw Joe Wilson.

Everything would be all right now. I tried to sit up.

"Stay put!" Nolan commanded. "Don't try to move too fast."

I obeyed readily, because the slight movement I'd made had caused the visible universe to cartwheel. "I'm all right," I said, a small lie. "Just shaken. And my wrist hurts." That part was definitely true. I tried to flex my fingers and winced.

"Think there's some swelling there by her right eye," Joe contributed, and when Nolan's fingers brushed feather-light just beside my right eyebrow, I winced again.

"I am really all right," I tried, spacing each word with deliberate care. "Just banged up a little. Let me sit up and get my bearings. How did you know I was out here?"

"Boze was barking his head off on your back porch, and the door wasn't locked, so I let him out. *He* knew where you were, all right. What happened, anyway? Railing give way?"

"Yes, but—" The memory of those eternity-long seconds just before I fell swept back over me, and I shivered. "It had some help. Did you—did you see anyone around?"

"Was someone here?" Nolan's voice was sharp.

"Someone pushed me. I'm sure of it."

Joe Wilson took a deep breath and stood up straight. "Real sure?" he asked, looking down at me. "Didn't see anybody. Though Boze was yapping like a coyote before he decided to play Superdog and come rescue you."

"I'm almost sure there was someone in the apartment," I insisted. "I went up to get some books that were in the window seat, and I thought I heard something but figured it was the raccoons, and when I came out—"

"Raccoons do not normally push people off porches," Nolan said firmly. "And I warned you those railings were rickety. You were darned lucky that there were sumac bushes right where you landed—probably broke your fall."

"Hit her head on that stump, like as not," Joe contributed. "Knocked her silly."

"I'm not silly, and I was pushed, darn it," I told them.

Joe muttered something about checking the apartment and escaped up the stairs while Nolan tried to defuse my glare by peering more or less professionally into my eyes in search, I suppose, of signs of concussion or the fires of madness.

I foiled him by closing my eyes. "I want to go back to the house," I said. "All I need is a little rest." I managed to smile at him. "Thank you for coming to my rescue."

"You're welcome," Nolan answered gravely. "But I

think we should run you up to the clinic at Lakeside for a checkup.''

''Absolutely unnecessary. I have a slight bump on the head, a tender wrist, and that's all. Please help me stand.'' I knew I sounded imperious and didn't care. I could hear Joe chuckling as he made his way down the stairs.

''No signs of anyone up there—and I'd say she sounds reasonably all right. Well, maybe reasonable has nothing to do with it, Nolan. But here, I'll give you a hand. We'll get her up to the house so she can be more comfortable, anyways.'' His walrus moustaches were quivering with amusement.

''You are a man of clear vision and intelligence. Thank you.'' I nearly told them that I didn't need both of them supporting me, but after three steps I changed my mind. I seemed to have lost the joints in my knees, and my head was definitely insecurely attached to the rest of me.

An hour later I felt as if all of the decision-making functions of my life had been taken out of my hands, and wondered how I could possibly feel both rebellious and relieved at the same time.

Joe and Nolan, discussing me as if I weren't there, had settled me on the prickly old parlor sofa like an oversized doll. ''Probably should call Doc Parker, if she won't go to the clinic,'' Joe said. ''She's a willful woman, isn't she?''

''Definitely. Yeah, I'll see if I can catch Doc. I'd feel better if he saw her.''

''I'm not going to a doctor. I'm staying right here.''

They looked at me as if they were surprised I could talk.

''You don't have to,'' Nolan told me kindly. ''He'll stop by The Birches.''

''A doctor who makes house calls?'' I'd asked incredulously, but they were already busily ignoring me, Joe saying he'd fix the window as long as he was here, Nolan saying he'd make tea.

Joe fixed the window and left with instructions to me to take it easy and to Nolan to take care of me. I'd managed to down the tea without snapping at the two of them, and Dr. Parker had come and gone and declared that I'd live. And I already knew that.

"I'm not worried about concussion," the good doctor—who seemed beyond retirement age, I thought—told Nolan. "But she could stand to put on a few pounds, and she looks tired. Probably doesn't eat right or get enough rest." He looked around him at the high ceilings, the shadowed corners, and gave an artistic little shudder. "Of course, living in this mausoleum just might put anyone off their feed."

"Hey, I'm fine," I told Dr. Parker. But he didn't seem to hear me. I frowned with exasperation. Nobody seemed to think I was capable of speaking for myself.

"Here," the doctor said, shaking a couple of tablets into a tiny envelope and giving it to Nolan. "Pain pills, if she should need them. May have a headache. You going to be here awhile?"

"Awhile," Nolan confirmed.

Dr. Parker nodded approvingly at him, then nodded at me with half a smile and some murmured advice to take it easy, and left. I was surprised that he could see me. I'd begun to think I was invisible.

"You don't have to stay," I told Nolan after the doctor's car pulled away. "I'll really be all right."

"I think I'd rather stay for a while." Well, all right—that was what I wanted him to say, wasn't it? I watched him across the dim room as he moved toward the tower windows, looking out at the gray afternoon, at the first splatters of chilly rain.

"Gloomy," he commented. "Getting cold, too." He

looked down at the card table in front of the window at the left of the tower and fit three pieces in my Maxfield Parrish puzzle, seemingly without even looking at them very closely. "I can build a fire in the fireplace in here if you'd like."

"That sounds like a good idea. Thank you."

"It scared the blazes out of me, seeing you lying there unconscious beside the carriage house like that." He said it suddenly and harshly, as if the words had been torn from him.

"I'm sorry," I said softly. "Believe me, I didn't do it on purpose. I'm awfully glad you came along when you did."

Nolan crossed the room toward me, and even in the dim light I could see the glint in his eyes, the set of his mouth. "I'm glad, too, Meg," he said, a catch in his voice. Would he reach out to me, hold me, tell me how much it meant to him that I was safe?

But he pulled himself up short, six feet from the sofa, glancing at his watch. "It's getting late—I'll just call Kate and tell her to go on home. Then I'll build a fire, and maybe I could fix you something to eat, if you're hungry?"

I shook my head slowly, and even that small motion told me it was beginning to ache abominably. Not food, no.

"Maybe—maybe those pain pills of the doctor's? There is a giant troll beating a drum somewhere inside my head."

"Poor Meg." I reveled at the tone of sympathy and caring in his voice. "Okay. I'll get some more tea and the pills and call Kate. Then I'll sit with you until you feel better."

And I wasn't sure I'd ever feel better. I still wondered what had really happened out there on the balcony—and I didn't want to be alone. Not now. Not for a while.

Still—"I don't want to take up all your time," I said tentatively.

"I want to stay. Unless you'd rather that I go?"

"No." My quick answer brought a smile to his face.

Fifteen minutes later a cheerful fire licked at the logs in the parlor fireplace, Boze was curled at my feet, the pills were already beginning to take effect. I was deliciously dozey, and Nolan came to sit beside me on the sofa.

"Lean forward, just a little," he told me, and—with caution—I did just that. It was worth the effort. His strong thumbs worked at the aching muscles along my spine; his fingertips massaged the tightness in my shoulders.

I probably purred. A wonderful lethargy stole over and through me with his sensuously healing touch; I leaned into him, so drowsy, so warm. . . . In a fading second of consciousness I felt his hands turn me toward him, heard him say my name. Heard him, from the edge of a cushiony, dark void, telling me softly that—heaven help us both—he loved me.

Blissfully, I floated into oblivion.

A strange sensation brought me back from that oblivion.

Hmmmm. My hand slipped over the familiar smoothness of my sheets, and my head—which I knew instinctively I shouldn't move too quickly, though I wasn't sure why—was cradled in the billows of my grandmother's old feather pillow. There was only an echo of remembered pain.

Then the strange sensation returned: a weight in the bed beside me, a touch on my arm. I managed to open my eyes—to complete darkness and wondered what on earth was going on.

Oh. "Nolan?" I tried, and felt, rather than saw, a stirring somewhere very close by.

"Feeling better?" Nolan's sleepy voice asked.

I couldn't answer right away. My, this was certainly cozy, wasn't it? "What are we doing here?" I finally managed to ask and wondered if the words sounded as silly to him as they did to me.

Chapter Nine

Acold nose accompanied by a moist whuffle nuzzled up against my ear. "Boze," I breathed, at the same time that Nolan switched on the bedside light and said with a trace of concern, "You mean you don't remember? Boze, for the love of Pete, get off that darned bed!"

"Yes, I remember. I think. You're still here. What time is it?"

Nolan yawned, glancing down at his watch. "Nigh onto the witching hour. And you don't think I'd leave you all by yourself, do you?"

"Thank you." A little uncertainly, I ran my fingertips lightly over my body, which at least was decently covered with the quilt that always hung over the curved footboard. Still clothed.

Wait—what was it I thought I had heard him say, just before I sank into a bottomless oblivion? Something about love? I must have been delirious.

"You really reacted to those pain pills, I guess." I made a face. Maybe it was the pills that had made me think I heard those words. "I had to carry you up the stairs—I thought you'd be more comfortable up here. I figured I'd stay until you woke up."

"I'm grateful. And starved." I was slightly surprised at that fact, but it was undeniably true.

126

Nolan's eyes lit with one of his rare but almost devilishly irresistible smiles. "I'm glad. That's a good sign. I'll go down and make you a sandwich—or maybe you have a can of soup you'd like? Hey, don't try to sit up too quickly."

He didn't have to tell me. My sense of balance took a momentary leave of absence as I pushed myself up on my elbows, but in a moment I had managed to swing my legs over the edge of the bed. "I'm doing fine, I think. I'll just take it slowly. I want to go downstairs."

He started to object, then shook his head. "Okay. By this time I should know better than to argue with you, shouldn't I?"

I looked at him in surprise. He was learning.

The stairs weren't too difficult to navigate, not with a strong arm to support me and a long, muscular body to lean against. I may have leaned a little more than I needed to, but one couldn't be sure when those pills might kick back in, could one?

He settled me solicitously at the kitchen table and set about heating up a can of split pea soup and digging the crackers out of the cupboard. I watched him, my head on my hands, wondering if that fall had addled my senses. I was growing truly fond of him.

Darn it, I was falling in love with him. And what about those words I'd thought I'd heard from him? Imagination?

Now what was I supposed to do?

"Eat," Nolan's voice cut through my muzzy musings, answering at least the last of my questions. He put the steaming bowl in front of me and moved over toward the fireplace. "I'll build a small fire. It's chilly in here."

"Mmmmm," I answered, borrowing a noncommittal sound from his own vocabulary. Besides, it was hard to say anything else with a mouthful of soup.

When he straightened and turned toward me again, a small

fire was burning cheerfully in the fireplace. But the warmth in his eyes had cooled. He'd put himself back in control.

I fought back disappointment, but it was for the best.

"Don't you want some soup?" I asked him. "You haven't eaten, either—it's been a long afternoon."

"I'll fix something when I get home. I want to make sure that you're settled down first. Is there anything else you want?"

I considered my answer to that question very carefully. Then, unexpectedly, the only thing I could think of was the books I'd been carrying when I fell—was pushed.

"The books," I said. "Oh, darn! I was carrying some books from the carriage house. They must be out there somewhere."

"We'll look for them tomorrow. In the light. It isn't raining, so they'll probably be all right. Important books?"

"I don't know. I think they were Adelaide Middlefield's." I looked up sharply at Nolan, remembering suddenly that he'd been going to check the story for me. "Did you find out anything about her? Did you get a chance to check?"

"Mmmmmm." He nibbled thoughtfully on half a cracker and absently fed the other half to Boze, who always sat with eyes full of hope close to whoever happened to be eating. I waited, watching Nolan's slight frown, almost holding my breath. "I found two news accounts. One said simply that a tragic accident claimed the life of Adelaide Middlefield and her father, Henry Middlefield, Jr. The other said—possible murder and suicide."

"Wow. Who was supposed to have killed whom?"

"The hint was that she'd killed him. That she'd been depressed and unhappy the past few days, acting strangely, and one of the servants said they'd had a terrible row the night before."

"I don't know why, but I don't believe she did anything like that. Not Adelaide. I feel almost as if I knew her. Could it have been someone else?"

He shrugged. "I gather there was no one to suspect of any foul play. There apparently wasn't anyone else around the house but the servants that day. The one report did say they'd gone over the carriage house carefully for evidence."

The carriage house. That place spooked me.

Max. What about Max? "Daddy" didn't like him. But still—

"You look skeptical," Nolan said.

"I have a feeling there's more to the story, and I want to find the truth. It's important to me—I'm not crazy, Nolan."

"Did I say you were? But you've been under stress, Meg."

"If you tell me one more time that I should go back to Minneapolis for the winter, I shall sic Boze on you." We both glanced down at Boze, who aimed the most unferocious canine smile in all of dogdom at the two of us.

"Sure. All right." Nolan looked down at the table, then up at me. "It would do you good to have a change of scene, though. We're going to have our annual Autumn Festival at the end of next week. It's one of the biggest bashes of the year. Farewell to summer—you know." He hesitated for a moment. "Would you like to go with me? We go in for costumes and dancing and silly games and lots of eating—"

"I'd love it." I hoped I hadn't said that too quickly. Maybe he was hoping I'd say no. But in that case he shouldn't have asked, and the smile he gave at my immediate response chased away my doubts. When he left a little while later, both Boze and a bright warm glow trailed behind me up the stairs.

* * *

At three-fifteen A.M., I put aside the book I'd been reading in a vain effort to lull myself to sleep and allowed myself to do exactly what I wanted to do. Which was to think about Nolan.

I didn't know whether I was glad or sorry that he didn't try to kiss me good-bye as he left. He looked as if he wanted to, a look that made my heart turn flip-flops.

All he said, though, was that I should leave several downstairs lights on, just in case—in case of what? asked that ghoulie that occasionally twanged at my nerves recently— and that it might be a good idea to keep Boze close by.

Also just in case, I supposed. And all good advice.

The house breathed quietly around me, as if it were keeping a silent, careful watch. It was an eerie sensation but crazily reassuring.

I glanced down at the book I'd been reading—a vintage Agatha Christie, one of my grandmother's favorites. I'd just reached the last chapter and discovered that the kind, handsome, wonderful man I'd taken to be the hero was in reality the villain, and the poor heroine barely escaped disaster. From the sidelines a nice, steady, strong man had emerged as the real hero of the story, gently rescuing the poor, deluded heroine. . . .

Now, *that* was not reassuring. If Nolan turned out to be a villain—and, of course, he wasn't—who could possibly emerge from the shadows to take over? Judd Patterson? Maybe Jack Darling?

I chuckled aloud in spite of myself. *Hey, this is Meg Livingston's life, remember?* No need for any proprietary males to hang around trying to arrange the details of my life for me. Although I was getting rather used to Nolan doing just that.

After all, I wasn't my mother.

There was more than one way to look at that particular thought. I fell asleep at last, confusion over the ramifications of admitting that I didn't have to let my childhood memories dictate my actions for the rest of my life giving me nightmares.

I wasn't my mother. She wasn't like me, but in my dreams she kept appearing and arguing fiercely with me, and with Nolan, and even with Adelaide Middlefield. At one point I had a fiery disagreement with Agatha Christie.

It wasn't a very restful night. What little there was of it.

Nolan called about ten-thirty, sounding obnoxiously cheerful and wide awake. I was still nursing my first cup of coffee and glaring out at what was, for a change, a sunny, brisk morning, with a questing breeze that cartwheeled leaves along the driveway.

"Feeling any better?"

"Marginally, I suppose. It was either a very long night or a very short one. I can't decide which."

"I was up at seven-thirty," he said. Hateful man. "Trying to take care of what needs to be done here at the clinic, but it's too nice a day to stay inside."

"Phmph."

"Ah, so she's a grump when she hasn't had enough sleep. That's a useful bit of knowledge."

"Useful to whom?" I asked suspiciously.

He didn't answer directly. "I just thought you might like to take a walk later on. I think it's time."

"Time for what? A walk where?"

"Well, if you're determined to stay in Caribou Bay for a while, maybe it's time to put some fears to rest."

"What on earth are you blithering about?" I knew I sounded witchy, but I couldn't stop myself. After all, he was part of the reason my sleep had been disturbed, wasn't he?

"How about a late lunch at Red's—say about one—and a walk along the cliffs later? If you feel up to it, that is. We won't go too far. But you need to see the beauty of the view rather than. . . . " His voice trailed off.

"Rather than constantly associating the cliffs with Doris Taylor," I finished for him, feeling slightly mellower at his sensitivity. I'd been cowardly, dragging my heels, avoiding the bluffs, and I should confront that particular nightmare and put it behind me. I should appreciate the offer rather than snapping at him. "I feel up to it—and you're probably right."

"I'm sure I am, and it would be better if you had someone with you rather than going back there alone."

I swallowed a funny lump in my throat—I think it may have been my pride—and decided to ignore his easy assumption of being so very right. Again. "Thank you," I managed.

He sounded very pleased with me when he said he'd see me at one. I think he was probably smiling as he hung up. I know I was. And then I remembered the feeling of being pushed off the balcony, and the smile faded. I rubbed my wrist and wondered and felt a little edge of fear creep back in.

It almost looked as if they were having a town meeting at Red's. The place was packed—people I'd seen around town, people I'd never seen before. I missed a step, propelled into the unexpected bustle and buzz of the place, but Nolan's hand on my arm pushed me gently forward.

"Over there at the left," he said, so close to my ear that a small shiver of warmth streaked from my ear to my toes. "Edina saved a table for us."

"Darned good thing," I hissed back, trying to ignore the shiver. "What's going on here?"

"Caribou Bay democracy at its best. Final plans for the Autumn Festival. Everyone gets a say."

"And *I* say," Red's voice rumbled from behind me, "that they'd better be careful what spikes they put in the punch this year. A little aquavit, that be hokay. Not too much, yah? You feeling okay, sveetie? Hear you took a bad fall yesterday."

Only Red Kaarinen could call me sveetie and get away with it. "My, how fast news travels," I said. "I'm fine."

"Got to be careful around those old houses. You vant hamburgers, I suppose, or am I yumping to conclusions?"

"Hamburgers," Nolan confirmed. "How's Kitty?"

Red growled deep in his throat. "Restless. Don't like all the cars roaring around today, and I'm too busy to talk to her. She needs a friend. She likes to talk. You know?"

He hustled away, leaving me feeling a little sorry for Kitty.

Nolan was staring at a spot near the door, frowning slightly. I followed his gaze and saw Judd Patterson laughing with a small group. He spotted us and smiled and waved, starting toward us.

Nolan's frown deepened. Was he, maybe, just a touch jealous? I smiled inwardly and decided to be especially nice to Judd—just to see what Nolan's reaction would be.

"You're looking pretty good," Judd said when he got in earshot, "for someone who leaped off a balcony yesterday."

"Great grapevine in this town," I said wryly. "Though I didn't exactly leap. And you look pretty good yourself." He did. He was tanner, more fit-looking than when I'd first seen him. He had a way of wearing casual clothes well, managing to look smooth and expensive even in jeans and a windbreaker.

"Thank you, ma'am. But just wait until you see me in my pirate's costume."

"Pirate's costume—" And then I remembered. The Autumn Festival was a costume affair. Oh, dear. I might have a problem there. But there were all those boxes of clothes in the attics—I could find something.

"A pirate's costume sounds fitting," Nolan was saying with a humorless smile.

Judd simply grinned and said he had someone to talk to and walked away. Maybe he'd thought Nolan would invite him to join us. That could have been interesting.

"What are you going to wear?" I asked Nolan. I was beginning to feel caught up in the idea of a costume party, after all.

"I'm going to be a fur trader," he answered. "Half Algonquin, half bear, half Frenchman."

"That's a man and a half," I told him.

"Right. You hadn't figured that out yet?"

Fortunately, Edina brought our hamburgers before I could think of an answer to that.

Forty-five minutes later we rounded up Boze from Red's veranda, where he'd been greeting people in his laid-back way. I thought about Kitty again, lonely in her special cage out back. But people just don't normally cozy up to a wildcat the way they do to an amiable mutt.

We left Nolan's van at Red's and walked down the road along the bluffs where Doris Taylor had fallen. It wasn't far, and the vivid early autumn brightness made the air taste like vintage wine. Small waves leaped and sprayed and hissed and murmured among the rocks at the bottom of the cliffs.

The lake was at its best—broad, blue-green, alive. On either side of the small clearing where we stood, the cliffs stretched away in the pure, shimmering air, crowned with pines.

Slowly, I walked about twenty feet north, scanning the shore below. There. There was the jumble of boulders. I'd been just to the left of it—

And she had to have fallen from just about this spot. I shivered involuntarily, the memory of those terrible moments sweeping over me, almost drowning the reality of the here and now.

From the corner of my eye, I thought I saw a movement beyond a pine nearby. Not a movement of anything with substance, but an insubstantial shadow that disappeared as soon as I looked directly at it. An unexpected shiver of fear made me take a step backward, my breath catching in my throat.

Nolan's arm went around me, his hand warm and reassuring against my rib cage. "Easy," he said.

"It's all right," I managed. That hand was more than just warm and reassuring. I leaned against him, and somehow his strength absorbed the fears and memories and left me conscious only of Nolan. Superconscious. And the slight, caressing movement of his hand told me he'd felt it, too . . . and then the hand dropped away.

But not entirely away, because he took my hand in his and held it tightly, guiding me forward. We walked close together toward a large, flat boulder at the foot of a gnarled pine.

"Okay now?" he asked, dropping onto the boulder and pulling me down beside him. We sat very close, just touching, wrapped in a sun-splattered little universe of our own— a universe that vibrated with unspoken words and needs and knife-edged awareness.

"It was just an accident," I said, my voice slightly uncertain. "There was nothing I could have done."

"I know that," he said soothingly. His arm had gone around me again, and I wanted to lean against him forever.

"I think I can put it behind me now," I said, wanting to add that doing that would be so much simpler if he were always beside me. But I didn't dare say that much. Not right now.

And that was dangerous.

"You won't forget it entirely," he warned me. "People don't forget things like that. And over the years the stories are remembered by everyone who was there, and grow a little, and become almost a part of a universal folk-memory."

"Goodness, you sound like a poet."

"Just another of my talents. I told you I knew all the old stories about this coast, didn't I?"

I snuggled more closely into the curve of his arm, hardly conscious that I was doing so. Somewhere a voice that sounded like the old Meg Livingston, the independent, emotionally uninvolved Meg, asked me just what I thought I was doing. I shut her out.

"Tell me about them," I said.

"Well." He leaned back against the tree trunk, but didn't loosen his hold on me, and I leaned back with him.

"Down the coast there," he said, "where that one bluff juts out, someone else fell once. The old story of the Indian maiden whose lover was killed in battle. She couldn't bear it and leaped into the lake. They say her spirit walks the bluffs at dawn just after every full moon."

"I like those stories, though I'm never sure I believe them," I told him. "But then," I added, trying to be fair, "I don't disbelieve them, either. What else?"

"Hmmmmm. Well, there was the canoe laden with furs

and Frenchmen that was swept out into the lake in a sudden squall. They were never seen again, though there are those who say they've seen a ghost canoe out on the waters when the light's right.''

''Maybe just after every full moon?''

He smiled and nodded. ''And then there's a more recent story, only about three years old. There'd been an armored-car robbery in Duluth, and the two robbers headed up the coast. They thought they could cut across the border unchallenged on one of the old overgrown logging roads—at least that's what we all figured.''

''They didn't make it?''

''There was a sky-buster of a storm that evening. The car swerved to avoid a rock slide and went over the edge. It was one of those times when the waves were nearly as high as the cliffs, and the car was swept out off the shore within minutes. They recovered the two bodies and about half the money the next day.''

''And the two robbers walk along the shore looking for the rest of it.''

''On the night after the full moon, probably.'' He chuckled and pulled me even closer.

''The rest of the money is somewhere in the lake, then?''

He nodded. ''Almost a million dollars. Believe me, there have been extensive salvage operations. But no luck. By now it's probably all reverted to tiny shreds that the fish try to feed upon.''

''You're being a poet again.''

He shifted a little, looking down at me. ''You seem to bring that out in me,'' he said.

I met his gaze, seeing the banked fires deep within those dark eyes. They were smoldering, glowing with a warmth that I wanted to lose myself in, wanted to meld with, wanted to carry within me forever. . . .

When his head bent toward me and his lips brushed against mine, the warmth became a firestorm.

"Meg, you are a witch," he murmured, his lips moving on my own and sending endless waves of intense yearning and desire through my suddenly boneless body.

I moved against him, my hands reaching up to tangle in that rich mass of dark hair and pull him closer. And he responded, the kiss deepening until all my old defenses crumbled into obscurity.

But there was, I realized vaguely, a voice saying, "Why?"

And it wasn't a voice within my mind; it wasn't the wind or the sound of the waves on the shores below.

Nolan groaned deep in his throat, pulling back from me. "Why?"

I sat there, hands clenched, willing the world to come back in focus. And not really wanting it to.

Nolan pulled himself to his feet, growling a curse, and I felt as if I'd been set adrift, alone, in uncharted seas. What was happening? Who was there?

The trees and boulders, lights and shadows, began to take form as I fought my way back to reality. For some reason, it was a painful fight, and I felt tears spring to my eyes unexpectedly. Impatiently, I brushed one away and glanced up at Nolan and then followed the direction of his gaze.

There was an amorphous shape half hidden by the tangled vines and shrubs—a shape that was becoming more and more solid and real and which spoke again.

"Why?" it asked once more.

Chapter Ten

"Otis!" Nolan and I both said the name at the same time, and the figure stepped backward, a look of alarm spreading over the man's childlike features.

"No," Nolan said firmly, persuasively, "don't run off. We won't hurt you. We want to help you, to talk to you."

Otis Taylor stood quiet, studying us. Then he nodded.

"Why?" he asked again, and there was a catch in his voice.

I could see him clearly now, begrimed and ragged, his cheeks haggard and his eyes full of pain. My heart went out to him. This childlike creature couldn't have meant me any harm.

"Otis," I said softly, "if you wanted to talk to me, I'm here. Let me help you. What do you want to know?"

"Why," he repeated yet again. "Why didn't you stop her from falling? You were here. You let her die. Did you push her?" Pathetic, accusing, confused.

The beginnings of understanding began to stir, wraithlike, at the back of my mind. Nolan took hold of my hand once again, squeezing it, reassuring but wisely silent.

"Otis, I wasn't at the top of the cliff. I was at the bottom, down there by the lake."

He looked past me, to the spot where the land fell off abruptly. "Down there? Not up here?"

"That's right. You didn't know that?"

"No," he said, shaking his head slowly. "But then why didn't you catch her?"

"I couldn't have, Otis. I was on the other side of a big boulder when she fell." Not to mention that if I'd even been able to try, there would have been two fatalities rather than one.

"Oh." His voice seemed to crumble on the word, and he began to cry silently, shoulders heaving and tears chasing each other through the dirt on his cheeks. "I'm tired. And I'm hungry. I wanted to find my mama; I wanted to make everything okay. It isn't okay, is it? And I don't know what to do now."

"I do," Nolan said gently. "Otis, will you come with us? Does a hamburger and French fries sound good to you?"

"And root beer?" Otis asked, and Nolan nodded. Otis's face brightened, and he came toward us trustingly. "Let's go, then," he said.

Boze fell into step close beside Otis, looking up at him questioningly, acting as protective as Boze could manage to look. And Otis paused from time to time to pat the dog on the head, talking under his breath to him.

We were halfway to Red's when Otis stopped midshamble and shot me a sideways look. "You didn't see what happened?" I shook my head. "But someone else besides me wonders, too. That man."

"What man?" I asked, startled.

"The one who watches. I don't know." He shrugged and seemed unable to answer any more questions, leaving me with a knot of fear in the pit of my stomach and my own version of Otis's "why's" chasing their way through my mind.

Nolan's face had turned tense and strained, and he put his arm across my shoulders. "We'll try asking again later," he said in a low voice to me. "It could be his imagination, of course."

"I suppose," I said, but I didn't believe that.

Less than half an hour later, the worst of the grime had been washed away in the kitchen at The Red Finn's, and Edina was clucking around Otis like a mother hen. Red was busy loading a plate to overflowing, talking to himself the whole time. It was hard to make out most of what he was saying, but I did catch the repeated words, "So vat do ve do vith him now? Poor lost ting."

The poor lost ting was being well taken care of.

But he didn't seem to know what Nolan was talking about when he asked him, carefully, about "that man" he'd seen watching Meg Livingston. He'd pushed that idea into some box in his mind and slammed the lid on it, and we couldn't get any more information from him. The only thing he was interested in was hunching over the small table at the back of the kitchen and shoveling in enough food to fill all the empty places in his body.

For the empty places in his soul and life, we could do little.

"I haff decided." Red's voice came from behind us as Nolan and I sat watching Otis. He handed each of us a plate with a juicy burger of our own and waved away thanks. "He stays vith us. For now. Until tings are straightened out, he stays vith us."

"There's enough room at the house for him," Edina chimed in. "The house" was their dwelling, set back 100 feet from the inn. I'd noticed it—a small, neat place, nestled in its own vegetable and flower gardens. A healing place for a hurt man-child. "We'll try to get hold of his father, and then we'll see what happens."

"No." Otis said and went back to his burger.

Edina and I exchanged wry glances, and she said softly, "We can only try."

I nodded grateful agreement. "Thank you," I said, and Nolan and I collected Boze from his vantage point on the veranda and drove, rather silently, back to The Birches.

"The books," Nolan said suddenly when he'd pulled the van up beside the front steps. "What about the books?"

"Books?"

"The ones you dropped when you fell. Did you get them?"

"Darn, no—I forgot entirely. How could I do that? Come on, let's go look."

I was out of the van and halfway around the curve of the house before Nolan and Boze caught up with me. Boze veered off in pursuit of some unseen small quarry, and Nolan grasped my elbow.

"Slow down," he said. "They're not going anywhere."

"How do I know that?" I answered fiercely, feeling suddenly overwhelmed by everything that had been happening. "How do I know that someone didn't push me so that they could get hold of those books?" The thought hadn't even entered my head until that moment, but now that it was there, it stuck like flypaper. "I know they're important. I have to help Adelaide."

"Now, just a darned minute. How can you help someone who's been dead for seventy years?"

"I—I want to clear her of suspicion of murder and suicide. I just feel so sure that there's more to the story. And you probably think I'm crazy."

"Of course I don't". He gathered me to him, and I was swept back into that world of longing. "But I am beginning to worry about myself." He kissed me, and the longing deepened: for what seemed an eternity there was nothing in the world except the two of us. The very forest itself seemed to be watching, listening.

It took a tremendous effort, but I pulled myself away at last. This wasn't the time or place. But I was sure now that there *would* be a time and place—and it would be soon.

He took a deep, uneven breath and relaxed his hold on me. "Oh, Meg, what am I going to do about you?"

I could almost smile, I was asking myself the same question.

"We'd better look for those books." I tried to regain some vestige of rational thought. "We'll figure out what to do about us later." *But when and how?* asked a little voice deep inside.

Nolan shook his head slightly and fell into step beside me. Silently, we scoured the grasses and shrubs at the base of the balcony, keeping a safe distance apart.

"Here," I said. "Thank goodness." Scattered under the branches of the sumacs were the books, the journals, I'd been carrying when I fell. I gathered them up carefully; the edge of the envelope still protruded from one. "We can take them back to the house and—"

The sharp report that cut off my words cut off my breath and nearly made my heart stop beating.

A gunshot. It had to be a gunshot, and not far away.

And a high-pitched bark and then frantic yipping—"Boze!" I cried out. I would have run toward the sound if Nolan hadn't caught hold of me.

"Easy," he said almost inaudibly. "The next shot might get you."

"But Boze—" I started, my voice thin. At that moment, breaking wildly from the underbrush with tail and ears streaming back, Boze careened toward us. I dropped the books and fell to my knees beside him. No blood. He seemed all right—trembling, whimpering, but all right.

"Be very quiet," Nolan said in an undertone. I looked up at him, standing there like a granite statue, staring in the direction from which the shot had come with a look of intense concentration on his face.

"Gone," he said after a long moment. "Toward the road." He looked momentarily torn, as if he couldn't decide whether to pursue the gunman or stay with Boze and myself.

Boze and I won.

"I don't like this," Nolan said.

"I don't care much for it myself."

"You're not staying here."

There wasn't much room for argument in either his tone or his words, and a flaring of my old resentment at his assumption of authority coursed through my mind briefly. And was gone.

"Where do you suggest I go?" I inquired sweetly.

He hesitated. "To the lodge, maybe. No, not to the lodge. I want to keep a personal eye on you. You're coming to my place, you and Boze both."

"But that leaves The Birches unguarded."

"If someone is determined to break in or to shoot you or your dog, I don't want you here. I don't know whether someone is after you personally or something in The Birches, but I want you with me. I could stay here with you, but I think you still might be a target. You'd be better off out of the house. We'll lock up as securely as we can here, and I'll call Jack Darling and tell him what's happened. He can keep an eye on things."

I didn't argue any further. He phoned the sheriff from the kitchen while I threw a few personal things in my overnighter, at the last moment adding the books we'd picked up at the carriage house. Within ten minutes we were in the van, heading away from my brooding old house.

An edge of guilty reluctance nagged at me, leaving the

house like this, but Nolan was right. Darn him, he was right.

I knew where the clinic was—a stuccoed building just off Caribou Bay's main street. I hadn't really stopped to think where Nolan actually lived, I guess, and was surprised when he pulled off the street just beyond the clinic, onto a drive that wound through a quiet cluster of pines. An honest-to-goodness log cabin stood at the end of the drive, a small, solid-looking home with a sheltered stoop of a front porch.

"A real log cabin?" Why should I be surprised? It suited Nolan perfectly. It looked welcoming, a rustic retreat for a bachelor veterinarian.

"I guarantee it," he said with a rather proud smile. "All hand hewn and hand fitted. I know, because a friend and I built it ourselves." He sounded proud, and I couldn't blame him.

A leaf-laden gust of wind tried to follow us into the house, but Nolan closed the door against it. Inside, the welcoming warmth of the cabin surrounded us like a blessing.

It was small, but as warm and woodsy and masculine as Nolan himself. Carefully chinked logs formed a backdrop for North Country prints; crossed snowshoes were suspended on the massive stone fireplace. The living room stretched across the front, and only two doors led from it— one to the kitchen, the other to a bedroom where a deep-toned quilt hung over the foot of a peeled-pined bed. There was probably a bathroom between bedroom and kitchen. And that's all there was to this compact log home. It reflected Nolan's personality—strong, solid, attractive.

Boze ambled across the room and collapsed with a contented sigh under a book-strewn rustic coffee table in front of a cushy sofa covered with dark green-and-brown plaid.

"Wonderful," I said. Nolan beamed.

"The fireplace is double. The woodstove heats the whole

house in winter, and those floorboards are two inches thick. I did all the cabinetry myself.'' Books lined the built-in cases, and I glimpsed an entertainment center.

"You're a man of many talents, Nolan Chase.''

"Some,'' he said, his hand on my shoulder, "you don't even know about. Yet.''

I realized that I was still in danger—but it was a completely different danger from that which haunted The Birches. A—delicious danger. I moved a step away from him, shivering slightly.

"You're still upset,'' he murmured and turned me to him to brush my forehead with a kiss. "You're safe now. Don't worry.''

I wasn't at all sure he was right. This was his domain, and how was I to fit into it? I should have gone to the lodge.

"Hey.'' He reached out for my hand, seeming to read my mind. "It's okay. Come on with me to the kitchen. I make a mean omelet, and you must be hungry.''

Oh, I was, I was—and for more than food. But, for now, food would have to suffice.

Boze's canine instincts recognized the words "kitchen'' and "hungry,'' and he shadowed us into the kitchen—an attractive, well-furnished room that made the kitchen at The Birches seem prehistoric by comparison.

Nolan and I worked together companionably, carefully avoiding touching each other. And he was right (as usual!)— he did make a mean omelet of eggs and ham and mushrooms and peppers and cheese. Half an hour later I finished off the last of my toast and grinned across the table at him.

"You should get a job with Red. Omelets a speciality.''

He looked pleased. "I expect I could rustle up a different breakfast every morning for a week, if anyone were interested.'' He stopped to think about that and then added quickly, "I expect you'd like some coffee.''

I agreed solemnly that coffee sounded wonderful. Watching him cross the kitchen with his long-legged, slim-hipped stride, I thought about a week's worth of breakfasts. And other things.

"Now," he said in a no-nonsense voice, pouring my coffee. "Let's try to figure out why someone wants you out of your house. Because somebody obviously does. Any ideas?"

"Not a clue. What's there? I don't think anyone's going to take a chance on sneaking in a moving van and running off with the furniture that's left. And what else is there?"

"Could you be what they're after, not something in the house?"

"But why? Why me? No, I don't think so. The only thing I've unearthed that's of any interest—and that's only to me—is the story of Adelaide Middlefield."

"Tell me more about Adelaide, then."

"I don't know much. Only what I've told you." I hesitated for a moment and then added, "But I get these hunches—and her story intrigues me."

He stared into his steaming coffee. "It would be pretty difficult to get to the truth of things after all these years."

"Yes. But I do enjoy a challenge."

"You make me wish I were a challenge." Was his voice just a little husky? I heard a tiny warning somewhere at the edge of my mind and tried to ignore it. He stared down at Boze, who was scratching an itchy spot behind his left ear and still looking hopeful. Then he took a deep breath. "So you'd like to prove she didn't kill her father and commit suicide—to clear her name."

"That's about it."

"You're a remarkable woman, Meg. In so many ways."

"Thank you, I think," I said, trying to make my voice light and normal. "Just for that, I'll help you do the dishes."

"No need." He caught the change in my voice and matched it with his own. "Hadn't you noticed the dishwasher?"

I should have seen it, should have known he'd have one. "Being a vet up here apparently is a very comfortable career," I commented, helping him stack our dishes in the dishwasher. "You're not lacking for much."

He straightened and gave me a long, level look that penetrated right to my heart. "Not for material things, no. . . . " He turned and rinsed excess egg from his mixing bowl. "But being a vet in this neck of the woods isn't that lucrative, not really."

I didn't know what to say, so I said nothing. "Our third great-grandfathers were probably friends," he said thoughtfully. "The Middlefields were mining, right?" I nodded, curious, not knowing what this had to do with his practice. "And the Chases were railroads. And they worked together here, back in the early days, and made their fortunes."

So there might have been a connection between our families many years ago. That seemed right somehow.

"You were left with an enormous relic of a house and no funds. And I was left with a legacy and instructions from a grandfather who loved this country. Not a lot of money, really, but what amounts to—to an almost sacred trust."

I was beginning to understand. "So you don't really need the veterinary practice."

"Oh, but I do. That was part of the trust. Granddad knew I loved the wilderness and the animals, and he saw that I had an education that would lead me back here to take care of them. I work with the university and the state in keeping tabs on wildlife populations and possible trouble spots, observing and recording, and I'm here for domestic animals and semiwild critters like Kitty who might need me. It's my life."

Those last words were so simple. It was his life. He could never be a city veterinarian. It might pay more in money, but it would never feed his soul.

"There's so much I don't know about you." I turned my head away so that he couldn't see my eyes. The more I did know about him, the more there was to like . . . and "like" was too mild a word.

No, to love. That admission seared a flaming path through my mind and body, and I felt perilously close to tears.

He reached one hand out to gently lift my head so that I looked directly at him. "You know more than a lot of people do," he said. "And, for the record, I can't stand phonies, string quartets, grapefruit juice, or computer games. But I love peanut butter, snowflakes, the wind off the lake, and my life up here." His eyes locked mine, willing me not to look away. "But there's been something missing. I think maybe I knew what it was the first time I met you. But I don't want to love you and then have to watch as you walk away from me. And that could happen."

"I know," I whispered. I didn't trust my voice enough to speak aloud. I took a small step toward him and felt myself gathered in once again, close enough to feel and hear his heartbeat. "I wouldn't want to just walk away." I lifted my head and let my lips touch his jawline. "There must be answers."

He turned his head, and his lips moved with a featherlight touch over mine. "Maybe we can find those answers together," he whispered.

At the door, Boze barked, asking politely to be allowed to go out. It broke the spell—for that moment. What I had always thought was my innate good sense returned to tell me to go slowly and back away. I didn't much like what it was telling me, but I listened. "Let's take a walk with Boze," I suggested softly, and Nolan nodded.

We walked hand and hand through the chilled late evening and returned to listen to classic jazz over that wonderful entertainment system of Nolan's. The music helped to fill some of the empty places in my heart, but it didn't answer any questions.

It was late when I felt myself dozing off with my head on Nolan's shoulder. He teased at the tip of my nose with his finger to rouse me. "You need sleep. Go tuck into my bed. I'll sleep on the couch. Is there anything you need?"

Oh, yes, there was, but I shook my head. I thought about all the things I wanted and needed for a long time after I'd snuggled under that beautiful deep-toned quilt—and I felt lonely. But it was best this way, I told myself firmly. For now.

Chapter Eleven

It must have been about eight-thirty when the thump of paws on the bed and a wet nose in my ear finally roused me thoroughly enough to face a new day. Even then it was a few minutes before I could shake the where-am-I fog that enveloped me.

I grabbed my robe and peered through the partly open door. Nolan was in the living room, staring out the window with a cup of coffee in his hand. Coffee. That was what I needed. A few minutes later, hair at least marginally tamed and the sleep washed from my eyes, I joined him.

"Good morning, sunshine. Bacon and eggs?" he asked. His voice was soft, his eyes smiling.

Together we fixed breakfast. There was something idyllic about the whole thing. I wondered if I were really awake.

I was daydreaming wistfully over my second cup of rich, steaming coffee about the possibility of staying here, just the way we were, for a day, or two, or three, or a lifetime, when the phone rang. Of course, I should have known that it would. Real life unfortunately has a nasty way of intruding into daydreams.

"Right, Kate," Nolan said to the caller. "Got it. Well, no, it isn't all that convenient, but if you can handle things there—" He gave me a crooked smile, one that teamed regret and love and inevitability in a disarming way. "Yeah, I'll give her a call. Thanks for letting me know."

"Veterinary emergency," I said flatly. From somewhere, in the far distant past, I heard the voice of one of my old friends saying "Never marry a doctor." She didn't say don't fall in love with a veterinarian. "You have to leave. What happened?"

"Arvilla Milne, out at Crowfoot Lake. She raises horses. One of her mares is in trouble."

"It's not foaling time, is it?" I asked a little grumpily.

He came over and put his arms around me, and we danced in place to lovely, unheard music there in the middle of the kitchen floor.

"Nope," he said after a moment, letting go of me before things could get out of hand. "It sounds like food poisoning of some sort to me. I'll go back as soon as I can."

"It would be better if you'd drop me back at The Birches. I have things I should do."

"I think you'd be safer here."

"It's broad daylight. No one's going to bother me today, I'm sure." All right, I wasn't really sure, but I didn't want to admit that. "I want to get back there—feed Boze, make up my grocery list, look for a costume for the party, go into town after my mail. You can come by when you're done. That shot could have been just a fluke, you know."

He sighed a mock sigh. "And pigs can fly. All right. As you so reasonably pointed out, it's broad daylight."

"Thank you, Nolan, for giving me sanctuary last night." We stood very still for several seconds, each lost in thought.

Then he shrugged good-naturedly. "My pleasure. I'll stop by The Birches as soon as I can." There was a promise in his voice. "Hurry and get ready, now."

I hurried. Then I saw the books—Adelaide's books—and gathered them up. I'd nearly forgotten about them.

"I'd hoped we could look at these together."

"Maybe later. We'll find time. . . . " *We'll find time for a lot of things*, his look told me.

We herded Boze into the van, and twenty minutes later I was back at The Birches. What would the town say when everyone found out—as they would, I was sure—that I'd spent the night at Nolan's house? I watched his car drive away with a small smile.

The wind had come up. It was a chill wind, full of whirling leaves and thin, lonely voices that cried through the branches and under the eaves. The changing barometer— at least I blamed it on that—made me restless. I'd thought I'd settle at the kitchen table with Adelaide's books, but I couldn't seem to concentrate. A few huge hard drops of rain that sounded mixed with hail pattered against the window. I made a pot of coffee, and Boze and I paced together, back and forth, watching and listening.

Finally I gave up, leaving books and coffee on the table and heading for the stairs. I'd look through those boxes in the attic and find something to use for a costume.

Boze stayed close to my heels, evidently a little nervous about the storm. And I was glad to have his company. In the attic, the noise of the wind and the rain was even more eerily insistent than on the ground floor. The air up there no longer hung quiet and still; now it moved restlessly, took on a life of its own, trailed living fingers across my neck and down my arms. I shivered involuntarily.

Don't be silly, I told myself, and started digging in trunks and boxes.

Within fifteen minutes I'd found what I wanted. The moment I pulled it out from between the old linen sheets it had been carefully wrapped in, I knew this was it.

It was a marvelous concoction from the twenties, an elegant shift of tea-beige and tan and chocolate. The plain, dark-satin undersheath was topped by a long beaded bodice of pale silk chiffon, the pearls and bugle beads tracing a lavish pattern from shoulder to hipline. Below that, darker tan sheer silk fell to a handkerchief hemline that rose and dipped and floated over the sheath beneath it. Long silk sleeves fell loosely to a wide band of beaded brown velvet that matched the brown velvet that banded the wide bateau neckline.

At the shoulders, caught with pearl clips, a multilayered full cape draped elegantly toward the hem. I held it up to my shoulders and twirled around with it: it would be perfect. It fit—it was mine.

It was Adelaide's.

That knowledge took over my mind completely and vividly. I had no doubt of it. I looked around me, half expecting to see her standing there, admiring the dress.

But of course she wasn't there. Not visibly, at least. Still. . . .

I placed the dress on its protective sheet carefully over the back of a wobbly chair nearby, took a deep breath, and went back to my knees beside the trunk. Just below the dress was another wrapped pile of fabric, and it was a beaded brown velvet cape, obviously made to go with the dress. And there were golden slippers made for dancing, tucked along the side of the trunk.

Adelaide was there beside me. She was smiling. She was dancing, and the air in the attic swirled.

All of this was just the storm, I told myself sternly. "I've found my costume," I told Boze, and he grinned at me in approval. Adelaide. She was so much a part of my life now that she was becoming an obsession—and I had to know more.

It was still raining, a windblown deluge. I thought of Nolan as I slipped down the stairs toward the kitchen, hoping he wouldn't have problems driving; I thought of the force of the waves beating against the cliffs and shivered a little.

There was a can of tomato soup in my pantry. Tomato soup sounded comforting on a day like this. Boze slipped under the kitchen table with a dog treat, his own brand of comfort.

I'd barely started heating the soup and digging out the crackers and cheese when I heard a sound that cheered me enormously. Nolan was back. That had to be his van, just audible through the furious noise of the storm. I ran to the front door, hardly aware that my feet were touching the floor.

But the look on his face when I threw open the front door stopped me with a sudden chill that brought me back to earth with a jolt. He had his own private storm in his eyes at the corners of his mouth.

"Why on earth did you go out there on a day like this?" he asked abruptly, and I stared at him open-mouthed. "Don't you know how dangerous that could be?"

"Go out where?" I managed after a few seconds.

"Meg, don't play games with me. Out on the cliffs. This is no day to see how brave you are. With the wind and the waves today you could have been swept away in a minute."

"But I haven't been out on the cliffs. I've been here."

He looked slightly uncertain for a moment. "You were seen."

"Then someone made a mistake. I've been in the attics." This was not the way I'd wanted to greet him. I felt deflated and cold and confused, and I didn't know how to react. "Who thought they saw me? When? *Nolan, I have been here.*" I moved a step toward him, my eyes searching his face.

He shook his head slightly, frowning, then reached out and gathered me into his arms. The chill I'd felt receded in spite of the fact that I was pressed against a very wet rain-coat.

"I want to believe you," he murmured into my hair.

"Believe me. It was someone else."

"That fancy red-plaid raincoat of yours with the hood. No one else has one like it, not in Caribou Bay."

"That's probably true." I took a step away from him. It was my turn to frown. So far this wasn't making much sense. "Someone was on the cliffs in a raincoat like mine?"

"Sid Berman was driving into town to pick up his mail an hour ago. He stopped at Red's for lunch, and I dropped by for coffee on my way back from the Milnes'. He said something about crazy city women, and of course that caught my attention."

"Of course," I said sarcastically, turning away from him to hide the hurt in my eyes.

He caught my arm. "Meg, I didn't say it, he did. I'm sure there's some explanation. Where's your raincoat now?"

"On a peg inside the back porch," I said. "Where it's been for about three days. It's all some kind of crazy mistake. Come on, we'll go hang yours beside it before you drip a flood all over the entry hall, and then—maybe—I'll share my soup with you."

"Sorry." He looked down at the drips and then up at me, and the "sorry" seemed to cover everything. Though I still felt hurt that he'd think I'd do anything so stupid as to walk near the edge of those bluffs on a day like this. . . .

Nolan paused to give Boze a greeting and then went through the kitchen door onto the small enclosed porch, shedding his damp raincoat and reaching out to hang it on the peg next to the one where my own plaid all-weather coat hung. I walked along beside him, ready to prove once and for all that my coat was dry and that I hadn't gone out and that the whole thing was just a ridiculous misunderstanding.

I saw it at the same time he did. A puddle under my coat, moisture shining on the shoulders. The world seemed to stop spinning; I stood very still, staring at it, unable to say a word.

"Meg?" Nolan asked softly.

I felt my face crumple, and I started to cry. It was the last thing in the world that I wanted to do, but I felt mysteriously threatened; my refuge should be Nolan, but he wasn't sure he believed me. I didn't understand any of what was going on—except that I needed him.

"Someone else must have been wearing it," I tried stubbornly, fighting the tears back before they could turn into hysteria. An attack of tears couldn't help my case at this point.

"Why? And who? And how—"

"Oh, darn, Nolan, I don't know! Can't you just believe me?"

"I want to. How long were you up in the attic?"

"Quite a while. I'm not sure. I was looking for something to use for a costume, and time just slipped by. I lost track."

"Long enough that you could have walked down to the cliffs?"

"I suppose so. But I didn't. Are you thinking that I had some kind of memory lapse, that I went down there without knowing it? That's ridiculous."

"I don't know what to think. It's a possibility, Meg. You've been under tremendous mental and physical stress this year. Things could be catching up with you."

"I don't have blackouts like that, Nolan Chase," I hissed at him, angry that he couldn't take my word. "I even remember that I stayed with a very gentle, caring man last night.''

"Oh, Meg." Nolan reached out and drew me to him. "I'm sorry to doubt you, but this isn't easy to understand."

"I know." I clung to him for a minute, then pushed away. "Let's go fix some coffee and try to figure this out."

But an hour later we were no wiser. Maybe someone was trying to drive me out—of my mind and my house both. It certainly appeared that way. I think I made Nolan believe, at last, that I hadn't been out of the house, but there was still that little edge of doubt. I even doubted myself. Had I blacked out?

"Sooner or later I have to go back to Minneapolis," I told him. "But not yet. And after I do get things straightened out down there, I'm coming back." I was surprised that I'd said that, but once it was said, I knew it was true.

"Are you, Meg?" There was doubt here, too, that tinged his voice with sadness. I knew what he was thinking—once I'd gone away, all this might look unreal, something that never happened. And he might be right. I had to do some serious thinking about the future—and, after all, Nolan hadn't asked me to stay, had he?

When he left at last, telling me he'd pick me up for the party at seven on Saturday night, I went upstairs and curled up in a tight ball on my bed and allowed myself to cry. And cry. Boze clambered up beside me and whuffled and whined deeply in my ear as if he, too, had tears to shed. Perhaps he did.

I tried to think clearly during the next day. It was difficult. It seemed possible that the Autumn Festival just might be a good-bye. And maybe that was wise: I should go back to Minneapolis next week and from a distance try to think this whole problem out.

It was a beautiful day, mocking my black mood, and I tried to busy myself with household tasks.

Trying not to think—too much—about Nolan.

But my subconscious mind continued to churn. And by two P.M., I'd come up with possibilities: it wouldn't be good-bye—just a temporary parting, nothing more. I couldn't walk away the way Chrissie had done. He would be my life—though it wouldn't be easy to give up all that I'd worked for so hard over the years.

And yet, in some ways, it seemed the easiest thing in the world. Those paralyzing cords of memory that I'd wound around my emotions ever since childhood were loosening and falling away. But could I convince Nolan that we could make it work?

Hope made me smile, made me dream. I put the candle holder I was polishing back into the cupboard and started to turn away when I saw the books. There they were, still unread, those last journals I'd brought from the carriage house.

It was high time I got to them. On the other hand, it was too beautiful a day to stay inside, and Boze was begging for a walk.

I compromised. It was just about a mile and a half to The Red Finn's. Putting on a windbreaker and tucking the books under my arm, I called an ecstatic Boze to my side and headed for Red's.

Boze willingly took up his post outside Red's door when we got there. Coffee, one of Edina's wonderful brownies, a window table, and an hour of browsing through the ledgers—it sounded marvelous. It was fantastic how much making the decision to spend the rest of my life with Nolan could lift my spirits.

The smaller booth at the end of the window was free. I

slipped into it gratefully, waving a hello at Edina, and started to stack the papers and ledgers in some kind of order.

Two unexpected things happened almost simultaneously.

One was that Nolan slid, rather diffidently, into the seat opposite me with an uncertain smile. "Good afternoon, gorgeous," he said in a soft voice. "Is this seat taken?"

I glowed at him but didn't get a chance to say anything before two glasses of water were placed carefully in front of us.

"Hi. Hello. My name is Otis, and I am your waiter." So meticulously spoken—so proudly spoken. I didn't breathe for a minute, and then I looked up at Otis.

"Well, hi." I had to stifle a giggle. Edina was standing behind Otis, making a funny face. "How good to see you, Otis."

"I keep telling him he doesn't have to be so formal," Edina said. "But he's doing so well."

"I'm helping," Otis said. "I'm staying. Red and Edina say I can. They're nice. Dad says I can. So I'm staying."

Nolan was smiling from Otis to Edina, but on Otis's last words he sobered a little. "You've talked to Mr. Taylor?"

Edina gave a helpless shrug. "More or less. You want coffee? Otis, go get the doctor and Miss Livingston some coffee, okay?" She watched Otis out of earshot, then added in a low voice, "No family feeling, that man. But it looks like we can keep Otis here. Like his pompous father says, he's a grown man and can make his own decisions."

A beaming Red appeared, looking ruddier than ever, behind Edina. "Besides," he put in, "you know vat that Otis can do? Ha! Otis can talk to Kitty. Kitty luffs him. He luffs Kitty. You believe that? Hooo! I never saw her take to anyvun like she takes to Otis Taylor. Makes them both happy. Is vunnerful."

He turned and went back to his kitchen, a trail of "vunnerful, vunnerfuls'' wafting behind him. I halfway expected bubbles to float magically along with him.

Otis reappeared with the coffee, and Nolan and I solemnly agreed that we'd like to have two large brownies, please, and when that was all settled, we sat gazing at each other over the tops of the coffee mugs as if we hadn't the slightest notion of what to say next. Which I know was true in my case, and probably in his.

"Nice about Otis," I ventured at last.

"Yeah."

"I'm glad you're here. I want you to know I love you." The words slipped out on their own, but there they were. True, too.

"So am I. What did you say?"

"I said I love you."

"Brazen hussy." But a smile had softened all the beloved angles of his face, and his eyes had a warm light deep within that would have melted a stronger woman than I. "What are we going to do with us?" he asked.

"What a loaded question! Give me time—I'll think of something. And, Nolan, I'm not going to walk away from you the way Chrissie did. Please believe that."

"I had already decided that I'd never *let* you do that. But—we've got to have a long talk, a lot of long talks, time to work this out, to be sure—but not here, not this minute."

I took a deep breath and nodded. He was right again.

Otis put down a plate with two enormous frosted brownies in the exact center of the table and beamed at us. "Anything else?" he asked and walked away, looking proud when Nolan shook his head and told him everything was perfect. I shoved my books to one side of the table and descended on the sinfully rich chocolate.

"Homework?"

"Oh. No." Actually, until I'd pushed them out of the

way, I'd nearly forgotten I'd brought them along. "I'd planned to sit here and browse through them. They're Adelaide's, I think."

"Well, in that case, I'm moving over to your side of the table and help. You have me curious about her, too."

"I doubt that we'll find anything," I said as he slipped in beside me. I was very aware of his warmth and closeness, and it was hard to concentrate on Adelaide's graceful handwriting.

But we did find something. We found several things—not proof, but strong indications.

"Max," I said, my finger on one passage. "Look. 'I met him in the carriage house again today when everyone was gone. It all feels so furtive. I wish Daddy would be more open-minded.' And here." A passage farther down the page. " 'Max was on the porch today when Betsy came to tell him he had a phone call.' Betsy. Who's Betsy?"

"Maybe the housekeeper. Keep going."

"Right. 'He didn't know I followed him in. And I heard him tell someone they shouldn't have called him here, and then words about Middlefield Mining stock, very low. He sounded angry, not like himself at all. He said something about Daddy's private records and that he could make an offer that would "undermine Middlefield Mining." He seemed to think that was funny and repeated it twice, and his laugh wasn't funny at all. Daddy's always told me I have no head for business, but this sounded shady. I wonder what he's up to?' Oh, what indeed."

"How naive could she be? Some things never change, do they?"

"Like greed and stock manipulation? Look, just at the bottom of the page. The last entry. 'Maybe daddy was right about Max. I'm going to tell Max that I know all about it, even if I don't. Maybe I can make him stop whatever it is that he thinks he's doing.' Sure, she could.''

''And what's this?'' Nolan had pulled out the envelope that stuck halfway out of the book, a yellowed envelope with faded script on the front that said just ''Adelaide.''

I slid the small piece of paper out. ''It's dated August 14. All it says is, 'Dearest, meet me at the boat dock at three. I'll explain everything.' And it's signed with just the initial M. Nolan, do you remember what day the papers said Adelaide and her father died? Wasn't it the fourteenth of August?''

''I do believe it was,'' Nolan said heavily. ''Damn. I never thought I'd be mixed up in solving a seventy-year-old murder mystery. Is that what we're doing?''

''That's what we're doing.'' And it seemed so right: it needed to be done. ''You know, it seems to me that the family fortunes started going downhill about that time, if I remember the stories right. What do you suppose happened to Max?''

''I don't suppose we'll find that out. Probably changed his name and went to the south of France to live in decadent luxury. Isn't that what crooks did in those days?''

''Probably. I'd be willing to bet he killed both of them.''

''It does look suspicious.''

The sun through the plate-glass window beside us was losing some of its brilliance. Time had slipped by, and I thought of poor, patient Boze, still sitting—I hoped—by Red's front door. ''I think I'd better get back.''

''Oh, gosh, what time is it?'' Nolan looked at his watch and straightened abruptly. ''I have an appointment at the clinic at four with one of the biologists from the university, and a shot to give one of the old timers' dogs. Can I give you a lift home?''

''Thanks, I'd appreciate that. George Baldwin's going to

call me from the North Star about eight, and I have a great deal I want to say to him. You're sure you have enough time?''

"For you?'' He squeezed my hand and gave me a look that would have melted steel. "The rest of my life. That is, if you're really interested.''

"I'm really interested,'' I told him, wondering why the room was spinning. Was that a proposal? I forgot Adelaide and George Baldwin and even all the strange things that had been happening at The Birches.

But not for long.

Chapter Twelve

My feelings of contentment, even of complacency, began to fade away as soon as I walked through the front door of The Birches. Something was wrong. The house was so quiet . . . but wasn't it always? Why this strange feeling?

Uneasy, I put my bag down on the library table in the hall. And a little gleam of dusty light picked out the pictures I'd grouped here, and it seemed to me they'd been moved.

A door to a closet was ajar. Just slightly.

I started through the dining room, being as quiet as I could, Boze close at my side.

Had a vase been moved on the dining room windowsill? But no, I told myself, I could have moved it myself when I'd last dusted. Whenever that was. Dusting was low on my list of priorities.

The kitchen—had the box of kindling by the fireplace been that far to the right? And there was a peculiar little gouge on the stone of the hearth that I didn't remember seeing before.

Boze went to the cupboard where I kept the doggy treats and gave me one of his hopeful "please" barks, and I relaxed a little. He certainly didn't act as if anyone were around. Not now, at least. But maybe while I was gone?

Nolan and I may have thought we'd found a possible answer to what had occurred seventy years before, but a lot had happened to me—around me—since I'd arrived here. I wasn't just being paranoid. We had more answers to find.

I had to think of something else.

Tomorrow would be the big party. I thought of Adelaide's lovely dress, hanging in my shower. I'd shaken it out thoroughly and hung it where I hoped its own weight and the humidity of the bathroom would smooth out the remaining creases and wrinkles of time. Trying it on, deciding what accessories to wear—maybe that would distract me.

Slipping it on, whirling in front of the mirror, I smiled. From her photos, I knew that we looked much alike, and I knew, in that mirror image, exactly how Adelaide had looked in that gown. She had been in danger, and danger was stalking me, too; I felt an affinity to her that reached out over the years.

I was ready long before Nolan picked me up at seven.

"A vision," he said, taking in every detail from my head to my toes and making my cheeks flame in response to the burning sparks of sensuous appreciation in his eyes. "Where did that outfit come from? No, let me guess. Adelaide."

"Right. And you look—well, a little fierce, if you want to know the truth."

"Fringed buckskin and wampum and bearskin caps will do that," he said with a mock snarl, "and not seeing a beautiful woman for months and months—you know what that does to a man?"

I could guess. As a matter of fact, I thought it might be fun to find out exact details, but we had a party to go to. "You can show me later, voyageur."

"Great idea. We could even skip the party."

"We'd be missed. Wouldn't we?"

"Probably, darn it. All right. Have you got a coat?"

I swirled my matching cape from its hanger on the hall

tree and gave him a full-fledged flapper pose. "What do you think?"

"I think you're beautiful. Let's get out of here before you vamp me completely." I thought that sounded as if it might be interesting, but I growled and grabbed his arm, heading for the front door. After all, our absence probably *would* be noticed.

The one and only place in town big enough to hold something like an Autumn Festival was the so-called "conference room" at the lodge. Compared to the facilities at the North Star, it was minuscule, and it was bursting at the seams when we arrived.

A kaleidoscope of impressions: exuberant decorations, colorful costumes of all types, a long, festooned table groaning under the weight of a generous smorgasbord, live music from the adjoining dining room with its dance floor—and where had they found enough local talent to make up a decent combo, anyway?

Of course, I recognized some of the people, even in costume. Red was a Viking. Jack Darling was a John Wayne cowboy. And Otis stood proudly behind the smorgasbord table bedecked in an Indian headdress that would have made Sitting Bull proud. Gnome-mama Edina worked beside him in a voluminous apron and cap.

"So many people!" I said to Nolan through the din around us.

"They come from all over the area. It's such a big party that some people even drive up from Duluth just to be here for it. There'll be plenty of headaches tomorrow."

I could believe it. Red was bartender, dispensing liquid refreshment jovially from behind a large bar, and I had a hunch he wasn't stinting on the aquavit.

Everyone knew Nolan, of course. A few people glanced curiously at me, as if wondering where I had come from;

mostly it was an accepting, friendly crowd, intent on having a good time.

And a good time it was—eating, singing, talking, dancing. I was caught up in the casual camaraderie of the party, having fun, laughing, feeling wonderful.

It felt even more wonderful when Nolan guided me over to the sidelines where an elderly clown sat watching the proceedings. "Someone here I want you to meet," he told me, and I detected a note of smug, controlled excitement in his voice. "Someone who has a seventy-year-old story to tell."

A seventy-year-old story—I looked eagerly from the Clown to Nolan, waiting. "This is Sam Tompkins," Nolan said. The clown nodded, his painted grin widening. "He's the one who brought his dog in for a shot yesterday."

"And Doc asked me if I remembered the Middlefield deaths in 1924," Sam Tompkins said. "I was only just nine, but I did remember, all right. Something I'd pushed to the back of my head over the years. I saw someone, you see."

"Saw someone?" I asked, my voice squeaking a little.

"Yeah, see, I was sort of an ornery kid—did my share of fibbing and fooling around. Used to sneak down across the lakeshore to fish from the Middlefield dock when I shouldn't. I was there that day." He fell silent, remembering.

"And—" I prompted.

"And I heard a fiercesome argument, and heard shots, and I dove under the dock. But heck, they used to do some plinking up there, no law against it. Still, I didn't want them using me for target practice. When I stuck my head out and looked up the slope, I saw this guy running. Wasn't one of the family—a young fella with slicked-back dark hair and the devil on his tail."

"But didn't you tell anyone?" I remembered that the reports had said no one else was there that day. But someone had been.

"Yup, told my pa. And he said I was fibbing and I was going to get in a lot of trouble peddling tales like that around, so I shushed up about it."

"Thank you," I said weakly, and to his pleased surprise I bent and kissed his painted face. Adelaide hadn't killed herself and her father. Max had—and arranged it so that it would look like a murder-suicide. As far as I was concerned, she was exonerated, and someday I'd take flowers to her grave and tell her that her name had been cleared. What a perfect evening this was turning out to be! I felt as if I were floating on air.

All that changed subtly within just a few moments.

Nolan and I had been dancing—a series of slow dances—and doing some gloating over our detective work. The floor was crowded, and we clung together, happy and acutely aware of the rhythm of our bodies moving against each other in answer to music that sprang from inside us as much as from the little group on the small bandstand.

The beat had changed suddenly, a little faster, a break in the continuity. I pulled away to look up into Nolan's eyes and was aware of a light hand on my shoulder that wasn't Nolan's.

A pleasant voice asked to cut in. "I'll return her to you in a moment," Judd promised Nolan. Judd, the pirate, whirling me away from Nolan. Over his shoulder I could see Nolan watching us with strained politeness. I smiled at him and gave him a little wave.

I'd be back in his arms in a few minutes. . . .

" . . . that dress?" Judd was asking as the music slowed. "Really a knockout."

I assumed he was asking where I'd found it. "In the attic

at the house," I told him. "The Birches is full of wonderful things tucked away in strange places."

"I'm sure it must be," he murmured, pulling me closer to him.

I didn't want to be closer. Something was wrong. It wasn't just my good old intuition—it was good old-fashioned common sense kicking in. Like a mule. Suspicions I should have had before—

"Is something wrong?" Judd seemed to have sensed the change in me. "Maybe all this noise is getting to you."

"No, I'm fine." I wasn't, but I was going to have time to think this out.

"I stayed on an extra couple of days for it, actually."

"Oh. You're planning on leaving, then?" And wasn't it high time he did? Why had he been here so long?

"Can't stay forever. I expect you'll be going back soon, too."

"No plans." It was best to be noncommittal. "When—when are you going?"

"Starting back down the road tomorrow. First Chicago, then Detroit. Lots of business to take care of."

"Yes, I suppose so." The thoughts whirling through my head made me feel a little sick. The name Max kept surfacing; it almost seemed as if when I looked at Judd, I was seeing Max. *Oh, come on, Meg*, I told myself. *Just because you're wearing Adelaide's dress—*

"Maybe I'd better sit down for a minute," I told Judd, not quite trusting my legs and wondering if I could possibly be right about what I was thinking, searching for reasons beyond reach.

"Too much aquavit?" Judd asked teasingly.

"I haven't had any," I nearly snapped. "No, I just don't feel like dancing right now."

Judd shrugged. "Whatever," he said. "It's been fun, Meg."

Had it now? I headed back toward Nolan with a small frown.

"What's up?" Nolan asked, catching the frown. "That guy say something he shouldn't?" There was thunder in his eyes.

"Not really. But I want to sit down. I feel kind of strange." I must have looked as pale as I felt, because Nolan led me over to a chair and sat down beside me, holding my hand.

"Too much excitement for one evening, maybe." Nolan looked worried. Maybe he was right. Maybe I wasn't fully recovered.

But—"No, I don't think it's that." I needed time to think.

"Goodness, you're looking kind of peaked." It was Mama-gnome Edina's voice, and she was peering at me anxiously. "Had a bad spell, did you? I'll get you some water."

"I'm all right, Edina. Really."

"Maybe you need to get back to town and get a good checking over by your doctor. He might be able to prescribe something."

"She."

"Pardon?"

"My doctor is a she. And I think I want to go back to The Birches. Now. I hate to miss the rest of the party, but—"

Nolan was already pulling me to my feet. "Good idea. Thanks, Edina. She'll be okay." As if I weren't even there. And I wasn't sure I'd be okay—not right away.

"What on earth is going on?" Nolan hissed at me as we made our way through the crowds to the front door.

"I'm not sure. I want to think about it."

"Judd?" Nolan asked suspiciously.

"Judd's leaving," I said vaguely. "Finally."

Nolan gave me a strange look but didn't ask any questions. And a half hour later I sent him away from The Birches after doing a Greta Garbo and telling him that I really did want to be alone. Until I'd had a chance to think this whole thing out logically and reasonably, I didn't even want to share it with Nolan. He promised he'd be back before noon the next day.

I lay awake deep into the night, thinking, Boze close beside my bed. I felt as if I needed whatever protection he could manage to give me, slight as it might be.

I hunched over my breakfast in a black depression. The long night hadn't given me any answers. Why should Judd be the villain of the piece, for crying out loud? It made no sense.

When Nolan showed up at the back door about ten, he looked as if he hadn't slept much, either. His eyes were shadowed, and the skin stretched taut across his cheekbones. I stretched out my arms, not knowing whether it was to comfort him or myself, and the deep wellsprings of sharing and yearning that flowed through us both told me that our need was mutual.

For a few minutes we simply stood in the middle of the kitchen, holding each other, wordlessly letting the warmth cocoon us against the outside world. Then Nolan pulled away slightly, looking down at me.

"Now. What was bugging you last night? Was it something Judd said? What's going on?"

I shrugged and leaned my forehead against his chest. "I just don't know—Judd didn't say anything. It was just a feeling, a strong hunch. Why has Judd stuck around so long? I don't think any of the local people are behind what's been happening around The Birches—and when you stop to think about it, who else is here? Judd Patterson. Well, Otis, too, of course, but we know he's not up to anything. Who is Judd? Maybe I'm all wrong—''

"No. I trust your intuition, and I've wondered myself. But it could be, I suppose, someone who's kept undercover during all this—someone we know nothing about.''

"And Judd said he was leaving today. Where does that leave us?''

"In need of a cup of coffee,'' Nolan said.

"Agreed.'' But even two cups of very strong coffee couldn't seem to give us any concrete answers.

"One thing I know. I'm going back to Minneapolis,'' I told him finally. He looked up sharply. ''I'll get some tests done, take care of a few things, and then I'm coming back.''

He reached over and put his hand over mine. ''To stay?''

"Do you want me to?''

"You know the answer to that. But do you think you could?''

City woman: could you live here? ''Yes,'' I said firmly. ''And it shouldn't take me more than a week to clear things up.''

"And your job?''

"I talked to George Baldwin the other evening, and I know exactly what he's trying to do. It would give me great pleasure to throw a spike in his spokes, believe me. And I think I can.''

"Come back to me soon. We'll make everything work, and with a little luck we'll find answers to some unanswered questions, too. Together,'' he said softly. I did like the sound of that ''we.'' By the time he left, promising to pick me up at six and take me to Red's for dinner, I was convinced he was right. As usual.

* * *

Now that I'd made up my mind what I was going to do, I felt a sense of urgency about tying up loose ends. My mind felt crystal clear, physically and mentally, I suddenly felt more normal than I had in months. My euphorious spurt of restless energy sent me up the stairs to start packing.

The sooner I left, the sooner I could come back. For good. It didn't take long to pack. I lugged three suitcases down the stairs and put them by the front door. I'd leave at dawn—I'd spend the evening with Nolan, a wonderful evening, full of promises. Full of love.

Boze pranced around me, his canine senses picking up my energy and translating it into a tail-wagging hyperactivity. By four, I figured a brisk walk would do us both good. Besides, I wanted to make one more visit to the dock, to the gatehouse. I had ideas beginning to stir in the back of my mind for the future; they would take time and planning, but maybe, just maybe—

When I came back, I found that I'd left the outside door to the side porch unlocked—but it didn't really matter. It seemed as if danger had slipped away now that Judd was gone, now that Nolan and I were making plans. Nothing would go wrong now.

Boze galloped into the kitchen with me, still as full of good spirits as I was myself. I went up to take a shower, thinking of the evening ahead. Thinking of a future I'd never have envisioned just a few months before.

I was still floating on my little cloud of happiness when Nolan came to pick me up. I put Boze on the side porch, where his food and water were handy, and greeted Nolan with an embrace that threatened to derail plans for dinner. And I stayed on the cloud during dinner—during Nolan's smiling words to Edina and Red that I was leaving but that I'd be coming back. Which Edina said she figured all along was going to happen. Inevitably, Red offered aquavit in celebration.

All was right with the world.

It shouldn't have surprised me, though, when—just as we were going to order dessert—Edina said that Kate had called. Ken Logan's mare might have to be destroyed. Could Nolan come?

This, I told myself wryly, *is also part of my future*.

Nolan asked if I wanted to drive out with him, but I declined. I had a few last things to take care of. "But stop by The Birches when you're done," I told him. "I'll take some of Edina's cheesecake with me, and we can have dessert there."

He grinned at me, a cheeky grin that told me he could think of other things for dessert, and we left The Red Finn's hand in hand.

He gave me a quick kiss and promised more later when we got to The Birches. I stood and watched him drive away, still feeling dreamy and detached. But as I turned toward the house, I came back to earth with a thump.

Odd. Had I seen a flicker of light against the birch trunks at the side of the house? Maybe from the kitchen?

Though I stared at the spot for what seemed forever but was probably just a minute, the light didn't come again. It could have been a flashlight, but it was probably just my imagination.

And where was Boze? I took a deep breath and tiptoed toward the side porch. Of course the smartest thing to do would have been to hightail it down the driveway as quickly and as quietly as I could, find the nearest phone, and call Jack Darling to report a possible intruder.

But first I wanted to find Boze. There was still the possibility—the probability—that it was just imagination. I grabbed a short stout branch that had fallen beside the path and tiptoed on. I'd get Boze and check things out.

I slipped up the steps and through the door to the side porch, frowning a little. Had I left it unlocked?

Then I stopped, frozen with uncertainty. Boze was stretched out next to his bowl. Not a nerve twitched. My heart began to thud. Was he dead?

Abandoning the branch, I sidled through the shadows toward Boze, the last few feet on hands and knees. He was breathing, but there was no response to my touch. Something was badly wrong. I had to get out, to get help—

The door to the kitchen opened. A man stood there, vaguely silhouetted against the faint light from the kitchen. For a few seconds the only sound was my own rather ragged breathing.

"Well," he said. "Back early. What a pity!" His voice was hard and cold.

"What have you done to my dog?" were the first words I could bring myself to speak. Then, "I thought you were leaving today. For Chicago or Detroit."

"You were supposed to think that," Judd Patterson said. "The dog will be all right, I suppose. Just a healthy dose of tranquilizer in his food. Nice of you to leave his bowl out this afternoon when you took him for a walk. I wouldn't mind if he died, though. I don't like animals." I'd known that, and for a moment I wondered how I could kill the man. "Get up—get in the kitchen while I decide what to do next. You've really caused me and yourself a problem, you know."

I hesitated, but he reached down and grabbed my jacket, pulling me to my feet and then shoving me roughly through the door into the kitchen.

It took a moment for me to register the details of the scene before me. There was a kerosene lantern burning to the left of the hearth, tools scattered around the shadowy room, and there was a displaced stone from the hearth. The cavity revealed between the floor studs was wide, fairly deep.

I thought of the cracks in the hearth and began to understand just a little—enough to know for a certainty who the man was that Otis said had been watching. Something was hidden in The Birches—and Judd wanted me out of there so that he could get at it.

And "it" seemed to be a large briefcase opened on the floor beside the stone that had been removed. It was packed full of—could that really be money?

"Beautiful sight, isn't it?" came Judd's voice from behind me. I turned to look at him; he was leaning against the doorjamb, a hint of amusement sparking momentarily in his eyes and then dying away, replaced by a marble-cold stare. "I suppose," he added slowly, "you could fall out of an upper-story window. With your history of instability, that just might fit in."

"You can't—"

"Yes, I can. I've waited a long time. Putting the stone back in place will be easy, and if you're not around to tell tales, no one will ever know, will they? I think we'd better go upstairs now."

It sounded like something I'd heard on late-night TV, but it was real. And Nolan wasn't here, and Boze was unconscious. Could I keep Judd talking long enough to find a way out of this? A tingling rush of adrenalin gave me a dose of desperate courage.

"But—how much money is there?" I asked, ignoring his suggestion that we go upstairs. Maybe I could maneuver toward the door—maybe Boze would come to—maybe Nolan would return sooner than I expected. Too many maybes, but I had to try.

"Over a million." His voice was hard, but there was an underlying pride in it. I took a step sideways, eyes fixed on the briefcase, hoping he wouldn't notice that step took me one foot closer to the kitchen door.

"Did—did you put it there, then?"

"Of course I did. Three years ago."

A flicker of memory became a flame. "The armored-car robbery. But you were supposed to be dead. Why did you leave it all behind?"

"I was badly injured, not dead. There were three of us in the car. They never tumbled to that, stupid cops. I ended up on the rocks, grabbed the case, crawled up the bluffs and found my way here. Not without a lot of trouble." His eyes narrowed. "You're awfully curious, aren't you?"

"Can you blame me? You've caused me a lot of trouble and worry, too, you know." I really was angry, and I glared at him, trying not to let the fear show through.

He didn't expect that. "Feisty, aren't you? We'll see how feisty you are after you've fallen from the attic windows."

"Those windows are stuck shut. You can't—" My momentary courage deserted me, and I sagged. "Why did you have to come back now, anyway?" It was almost a wail.

"I had," Judd said, enunciating each word as if to a backward child, "a broken collarbone, three broken ribs, a bad cut on the head, and a concussion. I just had time to hide the money before I passed out. And when I woke up, I had no memory, none at all. I left here in a mental fog, and—due to unforeseen circumstances—spent most of the next two and a half years in jail in Duluth. My memory has come back a little at a time. And I'm here now, and so are you, and that's all you need to know. Now I think it's time for us to go upstairs."

I gathered myself for a last-ditch effort to race for the

kitchen door. Judd caught my movement and strode forward very quickly to head me off. Too quickly.

His foot caught on the loose hearthstone, and he pitched forward, swearing. I dove for the kitchen door, streaked across the porch past Boze's prone body, dashed into the trees.

I could hear Judd behind me and ducked through a curtain of wind-teased creepers, thanking heaven for that wind— the tossing and whispering of the trees made it harder for Judd to track me.

Branches and undergrowth tore at my clothes and skin but offered concealment. I pitched forward over a log and touched the floorboards of the gazebo.

There was a break in the foundation latticing. I pulled myself through, huddling quietly into the darkness. If I could just stay still long enough, he'd take his money and leave. Wouldn't he? Or there would be enough time for Nolan or Boze to come to my rescue. I barely breathed.

I heard Judd thrashing around in the underbrush. And I waited. He wasn't giving up easily, and neither would I. Something crawled across my arm. I stifled a scream and brushed it away, and still Judd roamed through the forest outside.

It seemed like forever before things grew quiet. At last, hearing nothing, I edged out of the concealing dark—and immediately a small, dry branch snapped audibly under me.

Judd was still there. I heard him again, coming toward me, and I raced through the night in desperation—and came out, abruptly, on a grassy clearing that edged Lake Birchleaf.

The old dock and boathouse were just to my left. They stood out dimly against the dark sky. No haven there. And just to my right, only about twenty feet away, was Judd. He saw me just as I saw him, and I was trapped.

Nolan, I love you. If I have to die, remember that I didn't mean to leave you, not ever. Certainly not this way. . . .

Then I was out on the dock, running, the spongey wood and loose pilings swaying under my feet. As they were doing under Judd's—and I realized he was unaware of the danger. I heard a board give way behind me, heard him swear.

I stopped, gasping for breath, and grabbed at the rotten railing. It gave way in my hand, and I turned, swinging it with all my strength. He was off balance, and the railing struck him hard on the side of the head, and he toppled soundlessly into the lake. I stood poised, ready to strike him again, but I could see him floating motionless under the surface of the cool, dark water.

In the distance a dog barked. And from halfway up the meadow toward the house I heard a familiar, beloved voice calling my name. Calling me back from the edge of death.

Epilogue

Two weeks later a large group of us were huddled around pushed-together tables at Red's, eating Edina's wonderful apple crisp and sorting out the details of what had to be the biggest thing to happen in Caribou Bay since the Middlefield deaths. I'd just gotten back that afternoon, and I was surprised how involved and informed the town was.

They'd even been watching for me. Nolan and I hadn't had ten minutes to ourselves yet, with all the attention, a fact that was making both of us impatient. We sat close together, holding hands, something that was noticed, without comment, by half the town. Boze waited, patient, at his post on Red's veranda.

I hadn't been able to leave at dawn as I'd intended on that crazy night two weeks before. There'd been a few loose ends to tie up, after all.

And a lot of confusion. Nolan dragged an unconscious Judd from the lake, tying him with a bit of old rope from the boathouse. We had to check Boze over, call Jack Darling, return to the lake edge to drag a now half-conscious Judd up to The Birches. Nolan took charge, as was Nolan's habit. I was deeply satisfied to have him do so.

It was later that day when I left, after statements to the sheriff, after Boze and I had both had a rest. Boze seemed all right—no more brain-damaged than he'd ever been, at least. He looked apologetic. I tried to assure him it wasn't his fault.

"You look yust fine now," Red reassured me, pouring fresh coffee for all of us.

"I am. I had a thorough physical, and I quit my job." I smiled to myself as I said it. I'd talked to several members of the Board of Directors in a most persuasive way, and George Baldwin's old-boy network looked well on the way to being buried. A young woman whom I particularly liked was being watched closely for promotion. . . .

"Patterson's facing enough charges to put him away for a heck of a lot of years," Jack Darling said. "No plea bargaining on this one, I can tell you."

"I missed a little of the story, leaving that day," I said. "Though Nolan filled me in on most of it long distance." We'd talked twice a day while I was gone. "I'm still not sure why Judd didn't come back sooner, though I know he had amnesia."

"That's come out a little at a time. Talked to the police chief in Duluth yesterday, as a matter of fact. Judd hitched a ride with a truck driver back to Duluth after he left your place, holed up for a couple of months in a cheap apartment, kind of avoiding doctors and hospitals by instinct, I guess."

Nolan squeezed my hand and shook his head. "Surprised he lived through it."

"If he hadn't, the money never would have been found," I reminded him.

Jack nodded at me. "Instinct's what brought him through. Patterson—his real name is Jerry Peters, by the way—was a thoroughly polished con man. He started, almost by habit, working a few angles as soon as he was better. Got caught, though. And recognized as a parole violator. Ended up in prison."

"Where his memory started coming back," I guessed.

"Yeah. In bits and pieces. He came back up here the week before you arrived, but he still wasn't positive where the money was. He thought he'd have all this time to check out an empty old house and find it, but you poked holes in that plan."

"The man who was watching me." I looked up at Otis, standing behind Jack's chair, and he beamed at me. "He shot at my dog, shot out a window, pushed me off a balcony, and planted animal traps."

"And probably sneaked in and took your raincoat and walked out on the bluffs that day," Nolan said. "He was trying hard to make you leave, any way he could."

I sighed. It all seemed pretty unreal now.

As for Doris Taylor's death, it was pretty well accepted by now that it had been entirely accidental. But it had started a chain of events that I'd never anticipated when I'd come up to this quiet "retreat." Terrible events . . . wonderful events.

" . . . plans now?" Edina was asking, looking at both Nolan and me.

"A wedding between Thanksgiving and Christmas," Nolan answered promptly. I chuckled involuntarily. This was the first I'd heard of it. "Give everyone in town something to do besides watching the aurora borealis." I hadn't thought of that.

"And I think," he went on, "that all that money Meg's coming into—the $200,00 in reward money, isn't that right, Meg?—can be used very well to refurbish The Birches."

I stared at him, open-mouthed. That was the first I'd heard of *that*, too. How could he know before I did? Would I really get all that?

"A man was up here from the armored-car company last week looking for you," Nolan told me kindly, and I could see the laughter in his eyes at my reaction. "Jack and I talked to him, and he left some papers for you to sign, since I told him you were moving back up here and would be here in a few days.''

"You take a lot on yourself, Nolan Chase. Now I believe you want to marry me for my money.''

"Not quite, love, not quite," he said.

I couldn't quite stifle my smile at the layers of meaning in his voice, though I felt myself blushing. Everyone else in Red's must have heard what I heard. . . .

"And what's this about refurbishing The Birches?" I asked quickly, to cover my too-evident reaction.

"Oh, that's easy," Nolan answered. "With your background, we can make a good thing of a bed-and-breakfast inn during the season. And the carriage house can be remodeled into a fine veterinary clinic, you know. It would be very convenient, all the way around."

"You may not believe this, but I'd already thought of that as a possibility," I told him loftily. It was true, too. And I certainly couldn't let him think it was all his own idea, could I? "And during the winter, we can close up The Birches except for an occasional weekend and live in your cottage. I'm sure you wouldn't want to give up your cabin, would you?"

"You see how she takes charge of everything?" Nolan complained to the friendly group around us, a note of mock chagrin coloring his voice. "She's a stubborn, bossy woman, likes to have her own way about everything. I'm afraid she's going to be a real handful."

"Oh, I am, I am," I told him, leaning toward him so that our lips just touched. It didn't matter that it was a very public place; let them all get used to it. "You just keep that in mind, Dr. Chase."

And I kissed him thoroughly, a kiss that was fervently returned—to the enthusiastic cheers of nearly the entire town of Caribou Bay and an approving accompanying howl from a big mutt waiting on the veranda.